MYSTERY HORSE
AT OAK LANE STABLE

Also by Kerri Lukasavitz:

Gray Horse at Oak Lane Stable

Forthcoming books:

Dark Horse at Oak Lane Stable

Rudie the Happy Dog (picture book)

MYSTERY HORSE AT
OAK LANE STABLE

KERRI LUKASAVITZ

Spt. 14, 2022

Three
Towers
Press
Milwaukee, Wisconsin

Published by

Three Towers Press

An imprint of HenschelHAUS Publishing, Inc.

www.henschelHAUSbooks.com

ISBN: 978159598-798-3

E-ISBN: 978159598-799-0

LCCN: 2020950346

Originally published under 978-1943331888

Dedication

This book is dedicated to my mother, Kathleen, who shared her passions for literature, art, nature, and horses with me. I miss you.

TABLE OF CONTENTS

ACKNOWLEDGEMENTS

THANK YOU TO MY PROFESSORS at Mount Mary University: Ann Angel, Christi Seigel, Cynthia J. Salamati, Donna Rae Foran, Heather Sullivan, and JoAnn Macken, who encouraged me in graduate school to keep going when the writing got tough, especially Ann Angel because she believed in the rough start to a middle grade/young adult horse story that became this debut novel, *Mystery Horse at Oak Lane Stable.*

I want to show my love, appreciation, and gratitude for my family—for their determination and creative genius that has passed down through the generations. Thank you for your artistic talents, wild imaginations, and the dedication to work hard at your craft. Thank you for showing me that being an artist and staying true to your heart is a viable career path.

Thank you to my husband, Jeffrey, who tolerated many darkened meals when I was looking over a first draft or reading "just a few paragraphs" before checking the dinner in the oven, who has tripped over boxes of book orders, and everything else that comes from living with a writer/artist.

Thank you to my editor and publisher, Kira Henschel, for her knowledge and expertise. I was told

I was in good hands when I signed with you, but I already knew that from the first time we met. It was wonderful to discover you were a former rider and in-the-trenches show groom at the same stable I had also worked for. Your experiences around horses made this book believable. Thank you for wanting to publish this story after it was re-edited and sharing it once again with the world.

Thank you to everyone (including the horses) who were a part of the 25 years I spent around horses as a show groom, rider, and riding teacher. All of you were instrumental in my growing as an individual and as a professional equestrian, plus providing me with accurate details for being in and around a show barn—they make the story believable.

And thank you, my dear readers, for wanting to read wonderful stories. Without you, there would be no reason to write. Welcome to Oak Lane Stable. May you enjoy the ride.

—Kerri Lukasavitz

1

Saturday Morning

From down the hall, the kitchen wall clock cuckoo-cuckooed eight times as I sat and waited for what seemed, like, forever at the bottom of the stairs in our old bungalow house. I sighed.

The day I had been waiting for my whole entire life was finally here, and Mom and Dad slept late?

I had on an old pair of tan jodhpurs that were getting too small for me. The suede knee patch on my right pant's leg was coming off. I picked at a long, loose thread that was along the patch's edge, but all that did was make the patch come off some more.

Maybe Mom could sew it back on, or maybe I could finally get new riding breeches that fit me.

Dexter, my black cat with four white paws, played with the drawstring from the hood of my favorite purple sweatshirt that I was taking with me, that is, if we'd ever go. The sweatshirt lay in a lump on the oak floor near my striped stocking feet.

"It's going to be a super-duper day if they'd ever get up," I said to Dexter as I reached down and scratched him with both hands. I wiped off his shed fur on the front of my lucky T-shirt—the light blue one with the jumping horse iron-on decal on the front. It was tight and faded, but I loved it anyway. I smoothed the front decal twice with my right palm for double the luck.

I finally heard footsteps walk across the creaky floorboards above me.

"Dad!" I yelled as I jumped to my feet. "Are you ready? Are we going soon?"

Mom appeared at the top of the steps, wearing her new yellow bathrobe and slippers. She finished braiding her long, dark hair, like mine, and tossed it over her left shoulder. She came down the carpeted stairs toward me.

"Cassie, why are you shouting?" she asked. She gently touched the top of my head as she stepped around me and made her way toward the kitchen. "I need some coffee. Do you want me to make you some breakfast before you go?"

"I already ate some cereal," I lied. I couldn't eat now if I tried. "Is Dad up? Is he ready to go?" I tagged along behind her.

She plugged in the electric coffee percolator. "Your dad's getting dressed. He'll be down shortly. Are you sure you've had enough to—"

"Mom, I said I already ate." I lied again and sat down at the kitchen table across from her. I wadded up my purple sweatshirt in my lap and jittered my right leg.

"I know you're excited, but can you stop wiggling your leg?" Mom said. "It's making the table shake."

I stopped jittering.

Mom picked out a strip of yellow paint samples stashed on her side of the table, next to a stack of wallpaper books she put there last night. She held up the sunny paint color against the wall to see if she liked it. She was redecorating the kitchen.

"Do you want some orange juice?" she asked after a few minutes. The smell of fresh coffee filled the room. She got up to pour herself a cup. "I can get you a glass if—"

"Mom ... I'm fine." I sat back against my chair and flopped my arms down by my sides.

"Don't forget Grandma Leona is coming for supper tonight." Mom sat down and opened one of the thick wallpaper books. After she thumbed through it, she thumped it shut and then grabbed another one from the top of the stack next to her.

"I can tell her all about my new ... " I shot straight up.

Dad yawned as he walked into the kitchen.

I bolted out of the chair and ran up to him. "Dad! Are you ready? Can we go?"

"Hey, Cass, in a little while," he said after he hugged me and went to get a cup from the cabinet. "I need some coffee first."

I sank back into my chair. He sat down next to Mom, took her hand, and squeezed it. She smiled at him. They acted all lovey-dovey a lot lately.

Gross.

Dad started taking teeny-tiny sips of his coffee. First, he looked at Mom and then at me. I was pretty sure he was teasing me, but wasn't certain.

"I talked with Margaret at the grocery store yesterday," Mom said. "Said her husband lost his job last week. They didn't know how they were going to pay the bills if he doesn't find work right away."

"That's terrible," Dad said after he took another sip of coffee. "There are so many people without jobs. I wish this economy would turn around soon."

"We're so fortunate you got the promotion at work," Mom said as she reached across the table and squeezed Dad's hand. "We know what it's like to try and make ends meet."

Dad nodded and sipped his coffee.

I thumped my right heel against the chair's bottom rail.

Can we go now?

"Is the newspaper here?" Dad asked. "I want to see if there's anything about President Ford ending the Vietnam War."

My shoulders slumped. I slid down further in my seat. I looked at him.

Paper? Dad was going to read the paper? How much longer did I have to wait?

"Just kidding." He smiled and winked at Mom. "I can read it later. Ready?"

I got up so fast my chair tipped over. The clattering noise scared Dexter, who ran out of the kitchen. I picked up the chair and pushed it back under the table.

"Cassandra Marychna Lena Piotrowski, that's a new chair!" Mom said. She only called me that when she meant business. "Ed, make sure you are sensible about this. Nothing too big or too wild or anything she can't handle. I don't want her getting hurt." She looked over the chair to make sure I didn't put any scratches on it.

"Don't worry, I trust Stan Hoffman," Dad said. "He's been the manager of Oak Lane Stable for over 25 years and knows his stuff. I'm sure the places he's lined up for us today will have decent horses for Cassie to look at and ride."

"Just make sure." She looked up at Dad as he bent down and kissed her on the lips.

Oh, super-duper-gross!

I ran out onto the back porch to put on my brown paddock boots as fast as I could. I sat on the floor and put the right one on. I started to lace it up—

Snap!

The lace broke again. This was the third time in a week it had torn. I tied another knot and looked down at the cracked leather boots. I needed new ones. Dexter came to see what I was doing and wanted to play with the laces, but I wouldn't let him this time. I pushed him away.

"Come on, Dad!" I opened the screen door and let it close behind me with a bang.

"Don't slam the door!" Mom shouted from the kitchen.

I raced out into the yard toward Dad's new 1975 Oldsmobile Cutlass Supreme. Dad laughed when he got to the glassy midnight blue car. "It's a good thing the stable is only a few miles from here. What would I do with you if it was further away?"

"I can't help it." I buckled the front seat's lap belt. "I've waited for this day for, like, forever."

"Well, I wouldn't say it's been forever." He backed the car away from the garage, put it in gear, and drove down our gravel driveway. "You've been able to help out at the stable, and you've had riding lessons for the past few years."

"It's not the same." I looked down and played with my purple sweatshirt's zipper.

"I know you've always wanted your own horse, Cass, but it's been hard for us," Dad said as he turned on the car's AM radio. "I'm lucky I got the promotion, especially with the economy the way it is. I had to pay for the mortgage and for groceries and the dentist and the—"

"Okay, Dad, I get it." I sat up straighter.

We drove through the southeastern Wisconsin countryside where we lived. Black and white spotted Holstein dairy cows grazed outside in hilly pastures. Farmers drove tractors on the road as they pulled field equipment behind them on their way to cultivate crops they had planted. We passed farmhouses with rich-red milking barns and deep cobalt blue silos where generations of families had lived and worked the land.

The road curved around and through steep hillsides covered with maple, elm, and oak trees. Our neighbors waved to us if they were out in their yards and saw us driving by. My two best friends, Ingrid Svendson and Allison Greene, lived close by, just down the road from our house, but no one was home as we sped past.

And there were two small farms that had a few horses outside in pastures that I could look at on my way to and from Oak Lane Stable. Where we lived wasn't like the horse country in Kentucky or Virginia or New York, with their fancy estates that I saw in my horse books, but at least everyone was friendly.

"Where are we going to look for horses?" I asked, turning toward Dad.

"Stan's arranged some meetings with several owners in the area." Dad adjusted the radio's volume knob. Elton John's newest hit, "Philadelphia Freedom," finished playing and America's song, "A Horse With No Name," came on next. "He's lined up three places for us this morning."

I sang along to the song in my head. I still played with my sweatshirt zipper. I grabbed the door's armrest and sat up straight. The stable's large sign, installed by the side of the road and at the end of the blacktop driveway, came into view. It read,

OAK LANE STABLE

HUNTERS - JUMPERS

LESSONS - TRAINING - BOARDING - SALES

My chest tingled whenever I saw the entrance.

Hello, over one hundred acres of pure horse heaven!

"Will I get to ride?" I wiggled around in my seat.

"I suppose so, if the horse is decent enough for you," Dad said. "Stan's got a good eye for this. He'll let us know if one horse is better than another."

Dad turned into the long driveway lined with leafing-out oak trees and drove toward the barns. White fenced-in pastures ran along both sides of the drive. On my left, turned-out horses swished flies and grazed on the dew-covered grass that sparkled in the morning sunlight.

To my right, Joe McLaine, Oak Lane Stable's professional rider, trained one of the show jumpers, Night Hawk, over the cross-country course. The course's solid jumps were tough to ride. Only experienced riders and horses were allowed to use it. Those of us who weren't old enough to ride the course used a riding path on the left sides of the jumps but only if no one was training the show horses.

Just think if Night Hawk was MY new horse and we were riding over the cross-country course. His long strides would cover the ground as we'd approach the next fence. I'd settle my seat deeper into the saddle, tighten my knees and lower legs, and push my weight further down into my heels. I'd check my reins to make contact with his mouth. Then, with a powerful push from his hindquarters, we'd soar over the jump, land safely on the other side, and gallop off to the next obstacle—

"Looks like Mrs. O'Mally is coming down for a visit." Dad's voice startled me.

Mrs. O'Mally, the owner of the stable, was almost as tall as Dad. She wore a full set of riding clothes and was old like Grandma Leona. She walked toward the barn along a brick pathway lined with low bushes and brightly colored spring flowers. The path went all the way from her mansion's front steps to the brick pattern at the stable's main entrance doors.

Her troop of seven little dogs chased each other around her feet. Mrs. O'Mally had told me they were Jack Russell terriers. The terriers all had navy and light gray dog coats on (they matched the stable's colors). She suddenly stopped them and bent down. She pointed a finger at two of the dogs. It looked like they were biting each other's coats. She fixed the problem, and they walked on. I hoped I'd still be riding when I was as ancient as she was.

When we reached the pale gray main barn trimmed in dark navy, Dad found a spot to park among the other cars. We got out. Horses whinnied. An occasional hoof kicked a stall wall. Someone shouted inside the stable. Several women riders talked to each other as they came out of the open barn door with their saddled horses. Once mounted, they rode over to a small group of boarders who were walking their horses in the front ring where the hunt course was set up. They waited to start their usual Saturday morning lesson with Claire Ferguson, Oak Lane Stable's riding instructor.

"I'll find Stan." Dad walked toward the open arched doorway of the barn. "Morning, Mrs. O'Mally. I see you've brought the hounds with you."

Mrs. O'Mally and the seven terriers were nearly to the stable. The terriers played around her feet. Two of them ran up to me. They were cute.

"Good morning, Ed," Mrs. O'Mally said. "I have to bring them along. They get into trouble if I leave them unattended in the house. They've already ruined one of my best Oriental rugs by chewing off all of the fringe."

"Sorry to hear that. Well, I have to find Stan. Have a good morning." Dad walked into the barn.

"Hi," I said to Mrs. O'Mally. I patted the heads of the two terriers. They seemed to like it.

She smiled at me. "Hi, Cassie. I understand you have a big day today. Stan told me you're going to look for a horse. Remember, make sure it suits you perfectly. You don't want to make any mistakes with such a big investment."

"I'll remember," I said. "Are you going to ride this morning?"

"Yes, after I find out from Joe how Night Hawk schooled this morning. Have to run, dear. Good luck with your horse hunting." She gave a short whistle, and the terriers gathered around her feet. She and the pack of dogs walked off to meet up with Joe, who was still riding Night Hawk on the cross-country course.

I leaned against the car and watched the riders in the front ring. I took a deep breath. Mowed grass mixed in with oat straw and the woodsy smell of stall shavings. Fresh hay mingled with sweaty horses. Tack leather merged with citrusy fly spray. Heaven!

I heard the clomping of shod hooves. I turned to see a girl my age, slightly shorter than me, appear in the open barn door. Her neat blond braid ran down the front of her tucked-in polo shirt and nearly ended at the thin black belt buckled around the waist of her pale beige breeches. Her tall, highly polished black boots had a pair of smooth knobbed silver spurs strapped onto each ankle. She held her black velvet riding helmet in her left hand.

I clenched my teeth.

Great. Lisa.

Lisa Schmidt, my classmate and riding rival since 5th grade, led her showy chestnut horse, Go The Distance, outside. After she tightened the girth and pulled down the stirrup irons, she used the outside mounting block to swing up onto her horse.

Maybe she won't see me. Maybe she'll go over to the other riders and leave me alone.

I wasn't so lucky.

"Hi, Cassie," Lisa said with phony niceness as she rode toward me. "Are you going to ride today? Oh … that's right … you only get to ride one of the school horses for your lesson."

"I'm not having a lesson this morning." I didn't want to tell her, but it slipped out. "My dad is going to buy a horse for me today."

"You're getting a horse?" Her eyes widened first, then she squinted. "Get real."

"Stan's helping us look for one." I looked up at her and folded my arms across my chest.

Lisa looked down at me from the back of her horse. She rolled her eyes, pulled on her right rein, and pressed her horse with her heels. As she rode off toward the ring, she turned her head and said over her left shoulder, "Can't wait to see what you get. Probably some runt pony or a dorky donkey or a … "

I couldn't hear her last words. Lisa had turned to watch where she was going. She walked up to another girl rider who was sitting on her horse near the open gate. They both looked at me, giggled, and then rode into the front ring.

"Cass, let's go." Dad and Stan had walked out of the barn.

I made a face at Lisa she didn't see, turned away from the ring, and ran over to them. "Hi, Stan."

"Hi, Cassie," Stan said. "Ready?"

"You bet I am!" I walked next to them.

We went over to the stable's old truck and got in. I wiggled around to find a comfortable spot on the lumpy seat between Dad and Stan. By the end of the day, I'd have my own horse.

2

FIRST HORSE

WE PULLED INTO A DRIVEWAY with a tiny white house and a dark brown barn. The barn looked like it could only stable two horses. There was a three-strand electric wire pasture that ran behind the barn. Stan parked the truck near the barnyard, if you could call it that. A woman, who was shorter than me, came out of the house and met us outside. Stan introduced himself, Dad, and me.

"I'll get Master." She disappeared inside the barn's open doorway. She led out a dark bay Saddlebred that had to duck its head as it came outside. The horse was taller than Dad!

How could such a big horse fit inside such a small barn?

The horse was amazing. His coat was shiny. His mane and tail were long and silky. And he snorted at everything.

"This is Mr. Maestro's Masterpiece, Master for short. He's a champion show horse, just like you're looking for. Is this the young girl who's going to ride him?" The woman almost fell down when Master jerked on the lead rope and pulled her over to a grassy spot to graze.

"Isn't he a bit ... big?" Dad stood with his arms crossed, tipped his head, and squinted at the horse.

"Oh, no, Master is great for any size or level of experienced rider," she said as the horse again pulled her over to another patch of grass. "He's as gentle as a lamb."

I could tell I needed to train him better than she had.

"There's been a mistake," Stan said to the woman, shaking his head. "Thought you said you had a Thoroughbred. Cassie rides hunt seat. A 5-gaited show horse is for saddleseat riding and not for jumping. Sorry, he's not what we're looking for."

"Master can be ridden Western or English or anything," the owner shouted back at us since Master kept pulling her further away from us. "He's a great horse!"

"Dad, he needs some training and then he'll be fine." I touched Dad's arm and looked him in the face. "I'll work with him. You'll see."

Dad looked down at me. He started to walk back toward the truck. "Cassie, he's too big. He isn't the kind of horse we're looking for anyway. Your mother would shoot me if I bought that horse for you. Stan, let's move on to the next place."

"But Dad—"

"No."

"Thanks," Stan shouted to the woman.

Could she even get Master back into the barn?

I watched as the Saddlebred pulled her further and further away from the barnyard.

We climbed back into the truck's cab and drove off to see the next horse. I wondered why Dad didn't think Master would be a good horse for me.

He'd be perfect after some training. He's a little big for me now, but I'd still grow. I was only twelve.

3
SECOND HORSE

WE DROVE INTO THE DRIVEWAY of the second farm. Its sky-blue cottage with white shutters had pretty flower gardens planted all around it. A bunch of white outbuildings were built all around the yard. A long red milking barn with a white fenced-in pasture stood across the driveway from us. Two black-and-white Holstein heifers and a buckskin pony grazed together in the barn's front pasture. A woman with a wrinkly face, wearing a dark blue bandanna tied over her head and men's work clothes, came out of the barn. She met us by the truck.

"Hi. You must be Stan. Let me get Bucky for you." She ducked back inside the barn and came out holding a blue-and-white-striped lead rope. She went through the red iron gate and called out to the animals. The buckskin pony flattened its ears and moved in and around the cows to avoid her. The woman tried to catch the pony, but every time she'd get close to it, the pony would pin its ears, bare its teeth, and move just far enough away so she couldn't grab it.

Why was she taking so long? Didn't she know how to catch a horse?

"I've seen enough," Stan said. "Said she had a horse, but I can tell from here it's a pony. Bet you a dollar it's barely 14 hands."

"I've had enough too." Dad kept shifting from one foot to the other and looking at his watch.

"If that pony ever got loose, you'd never see it again." Stan pointed his right hand at the pasture. "How would you catch it? Look how sour its temperament is."

I saw the woman finally grab onto the pony's halter. "But, Stan—"

"She actually caught the pony!" Stan said.

The woman walked over to us, leading the pony. She huffed and puffed, trying to catch her breath. "Here ... this is ... Bucky. He can be ... a bit ... of a ... stinker to catch sometimes ... , but he's a good horse."

The pony pinned his ears, swung his head toward her, and almost bit her side. She shoved his head away.

Bucky needed a lot of handling, but I could fix him if I gave him enough love and training. It was obvious to me she didn't spend any time with him.

"Is this pony even trained?" Dad asked.

The woman shot back, "Of course he's trained! He was a champion many times when my daughter showed him. And he's not a pony. He's 14.2 hands."

Stan snorted.

"Thanks, but I'm not interested," Dad said.

Stan said, "He's not for us."

The woman gave us a sour look.

As we started to walk back to the truck, I turned around and watched her unlatch and slide through the gate. She led Bucky inside the pasture before she unhooked the lead rope from his halter, then jumped back. Bucky reared up at her. When he landed back on the ground, he pivoted on his hind hooves and galloped off, bucking as he crossed the field to rejoin the cows.

No wonder she called him Bucky. I thought she called him that because he was a buckskin.

After we got back into the truck, I said, "Dad, I could've trained him. She was obviously afraid of him. I wouldn't have been afraid. I—"

"You'd have had just as much trouble as she did," Stan said after he shifted the truck into third gear. "Why put up with an awful pony when there are better horses to choose from?"

"Cassie, I know you want a horse, but I'm not buying one that's dangerous. I don't care how much you think you can train them. Understand?" Dad sounded grumpy.

I would've crossed my arms across my chest, but I didn't have enough room.

Did Dad even want me to have a horse? I didn't get a chance to ride either of the horses at the two farms. Why wasn't he being fair?

"Okay, one more place to go before lunch. I hope this works out better than the first two. The man I talked to on the phone said he had several Thoroughbreds to choose from. Maybe we'll find your horse there, Cassie." Stan drove down the road.

I watched for pastures of horses along the way. I should've eaten something for breakfast. I was hungry.

4

HORSE WITH NO NAME

STAN PULLED INTO A LONG DIRT driveway full of deep ruts. He tried to avoid them, but I guessed there were too many of them. I didn't see the house and barn when we first drove in, mostly trees. I watched for them as we slowly bumped along.

As we drove around a tree-lined curve, the farm came into view. I noticed the house first. Its light-gray siding was falling off in patches, and the roof had holes in it. Heaps of stuffed black garbage bags poked out from tall grass that surrounded the yard. A once-red riding lawn mower had been parked under a tree near what was maybe once the garage. Rusted machinery was left deserted in odd spots around the farmyard. The old dairy barn had rotted and sunken in the middle—half of its roof lay on the ground. Most of the other smaller sheds had fallen over and lay on top of their spilled-out contents.

And then, I saw them. I covered my mouth to stop from crying out.

Four Thoroughbreds were standing in a muddy paddock next to the broken-down barn. Each one was skinnier than the next. I remembered reading a story in one of my horse magazines about a horse that was rescued from being starved. I wished I'd never have to see anything like that in real life. I wasn't so lucky.

My stomach felt extra-gross.

"Are we at the right place?" Dad asked as he looked over the dumpy farm. "Does somebody actually live here? What's wrong with the horses?"

"This was the address the guy gave me. Looks like someone's not feeding the horses. Wait here. I'll see if anybody is home." Stan had parked the truck and gotten out.

"Dad, can I go by the horses?"

"No. Wait until Stan gets back." He ran his hand through his hair. He didn't take his eye off of the horses.

I wanted to grab some grass for them. There was plenty of it around. Several bales of hay sat near the paddock too.

Why wasn't anybody taking care of the horses? Did the people forget about them? Would they like it if no one gave them any food? What was wrong with them?

Stan came out of the house with one of the shortest grown-up men I'd ever seen. He wore a blue-checked shirt, dirty jeans, a straw hat, and pointy-toed cowboy boots. They walked over to us.

Stan said, "This is Roger."

Roger's face had a deep pink scar that ran across his right cheek to the corner of his mouth. Roger smiled goofy. "Howdy, folks. Come on. I'll show you my horses. Is this the little girl who's going to ride?"

I stood by Dad's side. "I'm NOT a little girl. I'm twelve, soon to be thir—"

"Don't be rude." Dad gave me his "behave" look.

The horses were even skinnier than I first thought. When I got closer to the worn wooden fence, I could almost count their ribs. Their hip bones poked out, and three of the four had sunken-in eyes. Their coats were caked with the dried mud. I wasn't even sure I wanted to go in the paddock because the ground was so gross.

Would I ever get the muck off my boots if I go in there?

"I don't know about this," Dad said. "Do you want to do this, Cass?"

"I want to see them." I crawled in by the horses through some of the broken fence boards sort of fixed and tied up with laundry-line rope. I made my way through the mud. The sticky clumps made my feet feel heavy. It wasn't long before sweat drops started to tickle the sides of my forehead. I was afraid I'd lose a boot or, worse, slip and fall in the gooey muck.

The paddock stunk from rotting manure. I swatted away the flies that buzzed around me, and the horses, and a barely filled water trough that had green stuff growing in it. An oily smell came from a tractor that was parked inside the fallen-down barn, next to a pile of old rubber tires that baked in the sun. At first, a group of pigeons cooed while they roosted on the open barn rafters. But when they were startled by me, they took flight, flapping above me in a wide circle before landing exactly in the same spot where they had started from. I was sweating and breathing hard when I reached the horses. I heard Dad, Stan, and Roger talking to each other.

I tried to go over to the three skinniest horses that stuck together, but they kept turning away from me. I looked over at the bay horse who stood by itself. The horse had a wide forehead—a sign of intelligence—and large brown eyes. There was a small white star on its forehead. The horse softly nickered to me as I approached it.

When I reached the bay, I saw he was a gelding. He was smaller and in better shape than the other three horses. I ran my left hand over his neck and under a black mane full of burdocks. My forehead only came to his withers, so I couldn't quite see over his back. Since I was 5 foot, 5 inches tall, I knew the horse was around 15.2 hands. I looked down at his legs, but couldn't tell if there were any white socks— mud coated all four of them. The horse tried to swish flies with a black tail thick with more burdocks. I felt the dirty, brittle hair along his side. The bay turned and gently nuzzled my left arm.

My throat tightened, and tears started. I looked away from Dad and the other men.

How had my special day ended up with me standing in smelly gunk with starving horses? This wasn't how things were supposed to go.

I pretended to swipe at flies, but I really wiped off my damp cheeks with the back of my hand. I sniffed and snuffled a few times.

Roger said to me, "He's one of the better geldings I've got. He'll cost you $200. The others I'll let go for $125 each."

I gave the bay a final pat on the shoulder and made my way back across the paddock, each footstep heavier than the last one. I finally made it to the fence and climbed out through the broken boards. I wiped off the muck that stuck to my boots with the grass and weeds growing alongside the fence.

"Stan ... Cass ... a word, please." Dad motioned for us to follow him to the truck. "The horses are in terrible shape. I'm not wasting my money on one that's already sick. We don't even know if they're broke. Cass, we'll have to keep looking for a decent horse for you."

"But Dad, I—"

"There's no way I'm buying any of these horses." Dad crossed his arms.

"You know, the bay is a nice horse," Stan said. "He needs to put on some weight, but he's got a decent temperament. He'll look better once he's cleaned—"

"No, let's go." Dad seemed to have made up his mind.

Roger shouted at us, "Decide anything yet? You know, I've got a truck coming at two o'clock today. If you want any of the horses, you'll have to make up your minds pretty quick. One way or another, I'll get my money from you or the feed plant."

"Feed plant?" Dad shot a look to Stan. "What's Roger talking about?"

Stan cleared his throat. "He's talking about the pet food processing plant. The horses—"

"Dad! We can't let the horses go there! They'll kill them!" I grabbed Dad's arm. "Please Dad, can't we buy them? Maybe the bay? Stan thinks he's a good horse. He didn't bite or kick. He even nickered to me when I went up to him. You saw how he tried to follow me out when I left the paddock. He—"

"Cassie, no. I have to be practical about this. Stan, can we leave?" Dad walked over to the truck and opened the passenger door.

"I'll tell him we're leaving." Stan went over to Roger, they talked for a while, then Stan walked back over to us.

We got into the truck and started down the driveway.

I took a last look at the horses. The bay picked up his head and watched us as we drove past. My eyes filled with tears. "Dad, please. Can't we at least buy the bay?" I tried not to bawl like a baby in front of Stan.

Dad looked at the horses, then turned away. He dropped his eyes, adjusted the stainless-steel watch on his wrist he had gotten as a present from work, and shook his head "no."

As we passed by Roger, who was still standing near the fence and the horses, he smiled and held up his index and middle fingers on his right hand, with what looked like the peace sign.

I was sure he meant two o'clock.

5
HORSE MURDERER

AFTER WE GOT HOME, I TRIED TO talk Dad into going back to buy the bay horse, but he kept saying no.

"Why won't you save him?" I asked again. "Horses have a right to live, too!"

"Cassie, we've been over this a hundred times in the last few hours. Stop bugging me about this." He gave me a sharp look.

"You're a ... a ... a horse murderer!" I ran up the stairs and slammed my bedroom door. I flopped down on the bed and noticed my clock. It read: 2:37 PM.

Too late.

All I pictured in my mind was a big truck backed up to that smelly paddock, the horses being loaded up, and hauled away to a processing plant to become bags of dog food.

I couldn't stop crying.

Mom and Grandma Leona came upstairs. I sat between them on the edge of the twin bed with Dexter curled up by my pillow.

"Cassie, I know you're upset with your dad, but he's trying to look out for your best interest." Grandma Leona put her arm around my shoulders. Her pale yellow cashmere sweater was soft against my bare arms as she hugged me. "Don't be so angry with him."

"How can he ... just let ... those ... horses die?" I sniffed hard and gulped air.

"He said they were thin and sickly." Mom ran her hand down the back of my head, smoothing out my long hair. "We can afford to buy you a nice horse. Don't you want a healthy one?"

I nodded yes and pushed against Grandma Leona's side. I blew my nose with the handful of tissue Mom had grabbed from the box on my nightstand. I handed them back to her all soggy and snotty. She got up and tossed the mess into the wicker trash basket by my desk.

"Someday you'll understand why he did what he did." Grandma Leona gave me a hug. "Better?"

Not really, but I made a fake smile so she'd feel okay.

Why did grown-ups say stuff like that? When was someday anyway?

"Why don't we all go downstairs and have a dish of my famous rhubarb and strawberry dump cake?" Grandma Leona got up off of the bed. "I even brought a quart of vanilla custard from Leon's Drive-In."

"Okay." I still didn't feel any better and wasn't even hungry, but I didn't want to hurt Grandma Leona's feelings. "Come on, Dexter, I'll even give you a treat."

Dexter stretched on the pillow, jumped down, and shot out the door between our feet. At least somebody around here seemed happy.

6

SUNDAY MORNING

IT WAS SUNDAY. THE WORST DAY of my life. I still didn't have a horse.

I sat in the kitchen with my elbows propped up on the tabletop. I rested my chin on my hands and waited for the pancakes Mom made us for breakfast. Dad sat across from me and read the Sunday paper, which he had all over the table. I gave him my meanest look, but he ignored me.

"Elbows off the table and, Ed, put the paper down while you eat," Mom said to him. "Cassie, how many do you want?"

I put my arms by my sides and watched Dad fold up the paper he was reading. He stacked it with the other pages and put it on the empty chair to his left. Mom handed him a plate with bacon, eggs, and pancakes on it.

"Maybe just one," I said. "I'm not hungry." Pancakes were usually my favorite. Mom had made them to help me feel better.

"So, Cass, what are you up to today?" Dad asked before he took a mouthful of food. "Going to the barn to ride?"

I stared at him for, like, a whole two minutes.

Dad chewed his food and waited for me to answer him.

"Mom?" I asked as I slowly cut my pancake. "Can Ingrid and Allison come over this morning?" I looked at the forkful of pancakes soaked in melted butter and maple syrup. I watched the syrupy goo run off of them and back onto the plate.

Dad and Mom looked at each other. Dad shook his head and went back to his breakfast.

"Yes, but only after you first help me with the dishes and then pick up your room."

I was supposed to have cleaned my bedroom yesterday but hadn't felt like it after we got home. I took my plate to the sink, scraped the pancake into the compost bucket, and started to clean up the countertop.

After most of the dishes were done, Mom said, "Do your room first, then call the girls."

I hung up the towel I had used to dry the dishes. As I left the kitchen, I heard Dad say, "How long do I have to endure the silent treatment?"

Mom said something back to him, but I couldn't hear her. I was headed up the stairs two at a time with Dexter close on my heels.

7
BEST FRIENDS

I SAT ON THE FLOOR OF MY bedroom and leaned back against one of the twin beds I had for sleepovers. Ingrid sat across from me while Allison lay on her stomach across the other bed. We paged through a pile of horse magazines Stan had loaned me. I reached back and pulled off one of the purple, green, and yellow striped pillows that were on the beds. I sat on it to pad my butt since the room's olive-green shag carpet wasn't comfortable to sit on for very long. Dexter lay on the bed near my head while he cleaned his fur.

"How could your dad just let those starving horses die?" Ingrid asked me. "Why wouldn't he help them?"

I looked down at my magazine. "I don't know. He said he was being practical or something like that. I'm so mad at him. I'm not going to talk to him for a week ... no, maybe a month ... no, maybe for the rest of my life, or just until I go to high school."

"At least he's going to BUY you a horse," Ingrid said as she stretched out her legs from sitting cross-legged for a while.

"When? I thought I was getting one yesterday." I flipped through the magazine pages.

"It'll be okay, Cass," Allison blew and popped a pink bubble. "You'll still get your horse. Your dad can't be that mean. Hey, look at Sky Rocket. Isn't he a beautiful horse?" Allison leaned down and showed the magazine picture to Ingrid.

"I want to see," I asked.

Allison turned the magazine pages toward me. The photo showed Sky Rocket and his rider clearing a tall brick wall at a jump-off during a national horse show. The blood bay's legs were tucked up under him. He made the jump look easy. His black mane and tail flowed in the air. Two narrow coronet bands above his hind hooves and a forehead star were the only white markings on him. His rider had a big smile. I'd smile, too, if I was on my way to winning a major horse show.

"I wish my parents would buy me a horse like that," Ingrid said. "I'm tired of riding Bailey. He's so old. I can barely keep him trotting during a lesson, and he's such a putz when it comes to cantering. I want a horse that's a great jumper. We could win championships on the Junior Rider circuit instead of the baby Children's Division we're in now. When I'm finally fourteen, my horse and I could qualify for Nationals at the end of the season, maybe eventually ride in the Olympics as the youngest equestrian ever!"

"Dream on," Allison said. "Your parents won't get you a horse. I heard them say you're too immature to take care of one. Besides, Diamond Jack and I would beat you."

"Would not." Ingrid threw down the magazine she had looked at. She grabbed a different one.

"Would too," Allison teased.

"Would not." Ingrid twisted her hair. Her face turned rosy.

"Would too," Allison said. "You guys, look at this rider. Isn't he dreamy?"

All three of us leaned in to get a closer look at the boy's picture in the magazine.

"Kinda looks like David." Ingrid tucked a loose hair behind her ear.

"David Schaeffer? Our classmate? Lisa's boy-friend?" Allison asked.

"Yeah, he sort of does." I acted like it wasn't a big deal. I hoped they hadn't noticed I'd dog-eared the top of the page so I could easily find the picture again. I'd had a secret crush on David for, like, the last three years, ever since he moved to our neighborhood in fifth grade. I'd wanted to pass a note around class to find out if David liked me or like-liked me, but I was afraid of what he might say. Besides, he didn't notice me. He liked Lisa.

"Why does he go steady with her?" asked Ingrid.

"I don't know. She isn't even pretty or nice or anything," Allison said.

"Maybe she does things with him, you know, kiss, and those kinds of things!" Ingrid's eyes got big.

"Ew! Super-gross!" I changed the subject. "Do you think I'll win any of my classes this year at Shady Creek Stable's schooling show?"

"Probably. You always do great." Allison popped a bubble and paged through the last horse magazine from the stack.

I loved my friends. They were the only girls left in my class, except Lisa, who still rode and hung out around the stable. Most of my other friends from school had already traded in loving horses for loving boys, clothes, and makeup. Seventh grade was hard. Things had changed so fast. I was glad the school year was almost over. I had summer vacation to spend at the stable with Allison and Ingrid. We'd have a great summer vacation together. We always did.

"Come on, let's go to the barn," Allison said as she got up from the floor. "My butt's getting sore."

"Mine too." Ingrid straightened out the piles of magazines before we put them away.

"I don't want to go to the barn yet. I—"

"Awe, come on," Allison said. "I'll let you ride Diamond Jack."

They both looked at me and waited for my answer.

"I ... I guess so." I didn't need to go, but they wanted me to.

"You'll see. You'll feel better once you're there." Allison grabbed my hand and helped me up.

We left the bedroom and headed downstairs to tell Mom where we were going.

8
THE SURPRISE

ALLISON, INGRID, AND I PEDALED our bikes down our gravel driveway and turned right onto the country road that we lived on. A red tractor pulled out of a hay field to our left. It was about the only traffic we had on the road, except for the people who lived around us. We passed Ingrid's house, which was the next driveway down the road from mine. Her mom was outside digging in the front yard. It looked like she was planting some summer flowers.

"Hi, Mrs. Svendson," Allison and I said.

"Hi, Mom," Ingrid said.

She waved to us and went back to her gardening.

We rode along the curves and coasted down small hills. Allison was out in front, I was in the middle, and Ingrid brought up the rear behind me. We passed what used to be the Schultz's dairy farm. The land had been sold and turned into Arrowhead Acres subdivision. Allison and her parents lived there, but we couldn't see her house from the road. David and his family lived on the corner lot on her street, but closer to the subdivision's entrance by the main road. I wanted to see if he was outside, but we flew past his house.

Oak Lane Stable's sign appeared after the last curve. We coasted into the long driveway and pedaled smoothly on the blacktop surface. The leafing-out oak trees that lined the drive barely shaded us from the unusually warm late May temps.

"Look at Cisco, Missy, and Sir John chasing each other." I said. The horses were in the large pasture to our left. They thundered past us with their tails high in the air.

"They're beautiful," Ingrid said. "I want to ride that fast."

"You'd be afraid." Allison popped a pink bubble.

"Would not," Ingrid said.

"Would too." Allison teased her.

"Would not!" Ingrid scowled. Her cheeks turned darker pink. "And I want to ride on the cross-country course."

We biked past the cross-country course on our right. Joe, the professional rider, was schooling a big steel-gray hunter while Claire, the riding instructor, sat on Night Hawk out in the field. She must have been helping to train the gray horse Joe was riding after she had worked Night Hawk. It took a lot of guts and years of practice to ride those sturdy fences. I'd been riding at Oak Lane Stable for four years and could only jump 2-foot, 3- or 6-inch rail fences in the schooling ring.

As we biked down the driveway, I watched the steel-gray hunter take the fences as Claire gave

Kerri Lukasavitz

instructions to Joe. It would be a few years before I could handle jumping the 3- and 4-foot high wooden fences that made up the obstacles on the cross-country course. I hoped having my own well-trained show horse would help me to move up to riding bigger fences faster.

"It'll be a while before I can ride the cross-country course," I said as we pulled up to the barn. "Claire said I'm improving my jump approaches, but I could use more practice. I need a better horse than old George. He's such a spaz!"

"He's a slouch when it comes to lessons," said Allison, putting down the kickstand after getting off her bike. She popped a huge bubble that got caught on her chin. She pulled the pink goo off her skin, put it back in her mouth, and chewed again. "I'm glad I've got my own horse, Diamond Jack. Let's get a soda from the clubroom. I'm thirsty."

"So am I." I parked my bike next to hers. My T-shirt stuck to my back from the ride and the sun's heat.

"I need one too." Ingrid dumped her bike onto the ground.

There were only a few cars in the parking lot. I noticed two riders working their horses in the front ring. I turned back to Allison and Ingrid. I hoped Lisa wasn't coming today, especially since I didn't have a horse yet.

Just before we walked into the barn's open double doorway, we were met by the chubby boarder, Mrs. Wagner, who barely came up to my shoulder, as she led her 14.3-hands-high, chubby dappled-gray mare outside.

"Hi, girls," Mrs. Wagner said.

"Hi," we said together.

"Can one of you help me?" she asked. "I need someone to hold my mare. You know how she moves off before I can get on her."

"I'll help," I said.

"Cassie, you're a dear," Mrs. Wagner said.

I walked with Mrs. Wagner and her mare over to the mounting block. She tightened the girth, which took lots of effort. She pulled down her stirrup irons and stepped up onto the block.

"Just keep her from moving away until I swing my leg over her." Mrs. Wagner gathered the reins in her left hand. I held the reins by the horse's bit. She put her left foot in the stirrup iron and pushed off with her right foot. She swung over the mares back and plopped down in the saddle.

"Whoa, girl," I said to the pudgy gray mare as she tried to move under and away from Mrs. Wagner's ungraceful seat.

"It's okay, I've got her now." Mrs. Wagner pulled back on the reins. She adjusted her saddle and rode off toward the other riders in the front ring.

"Have a good ride," I said, turned, and walked into the barn.

My eyes adjusted from the bright morning sunlight to the barn's darker interior. It was cooler in the barn than being outside. A breeze drifted down the aisles from the open double doors at each end of the barn. The cooler air felt good against my sweaty skin.

The indoor riding ring was straight ahead of me, across from the main doors. The ring was large enough for a full-size jumping course. A man cantered a chestnut horse from inside the ring and past the open door of the indoor ring. The horse's hooves sent oiled dirt against the wooden interior wall. I heard him shout something to someone in the ring, but I couldn't make out the words because he went by so fast.

A fancy brick pattern paved the barn's main entrance and ran up to the indoor arena's doorway. Stan had called it a herringbone pattern. The rest of the barn's long floor aisles on my right and on my left were made of gray concrete.

A horse kicked its stall wall.

"Knock it off!" a man shouted from inside the stall.

The horse kicked again.

"I said knock it off!" he shouted again.

Quiet.

Keith Hintz, one of Oak Lane Stable's show grooms, worked on a boarder's horse fastened to cross-ties near the end of the barn aisle to my right. Keith stood on a wooden box and pulled the horse's mane to shorten it so it was easier to make into tiny braids for shows. Small clumps of pulled-out hair lay on the floor around his box.

The aisle where Keith worked had two rows of twelve box stalls on both sides. Each stall had navy iron vertical bars around its perimeter, above the wooden half walls, and a small window on the barn's outside walls so there was extra light to see with. That side of the barn housed Oak Lane Stable's horses and several boarders' show horses, including Lisa's chestnut. Every stall door had a brass hook for a leather halter and a rectangular navy brass nameplate.

Keith stepped down off his box and went into the tack room where the saddles, bridles, and other riding equipment were stored. The tack room was midway down the aisle and directly across from the wash stall used to bathe the horses. Keith came out with a brush and walked back over to the horse he was working on.

"Hi, Cassie," Keith said after he saw me standing in the barn.

"Hi." I waved to him and joined Ingrid and Allison, who were on the left aisle.

The left side of the barn looked exactly the same as the aisle where Keith worked, except there was a clubroom with comfy chairs to sit in and a big window to watch people ride in the indoor ring. Stan's office was next to the indoor arena's door and at the front of the right side aisle. The stalls in the left aisle housed school horses and several boarders' show horses, including Allison's horse, Diamond Jack.

Hooves clattered on the concrete floor. I turned to see the man who had been riding in the indoor ring come into the barn leading his chestnut horse. A woman walked by his side.

"He worked great today," the man said as he patted the horse's sweaty neck.

"A good effort," she said.

"Did you see him take the wall?" he asked.

"Jumped it clean," she said. "Later this week we can take him ..."

I couldn't make out what they said as they moved away from me. The couple walked down the aisle past Keith, who still pulled the show horse's mane. The rider put his chestnut horse on another set of cross-ties and started to untack his horse.

I could tell by the number of open stall doors throughout the barn that most of the horses were either turned-out or being ridden. Bob, the stable's head maintenance man, and his two helpers cleaned out the last few school horse stalls at the end of the left side aisle. The gray tractor puffed dark diesel smoke when Bob started it. My eyes watered, and I coughed. He drove it forward to the next open stall doors and turned off the motor. The manure spreader was almost full. The heavy odor of manure, soiled straw bedding, and horse pee filled the barn aisle. Allison and Ingrid stood near Diamond Jack's cleaned stall.

"Hello, Beauty Boy," Allison said. The tall Thoroughbred nickered when he reached his head out over the stall door. She removed a carrot piece from her pocket. His soft lips took it from her palm. "Ready for a ride?" Here ... let me put you on cross-ties. Ingrid, can you grab my grooming box from the tack room?"

"Sure," Ingrid said and walked to the back tack room.

Allison opened the bottom door and ducked inside with Diamond Jack's halter. She put it on him and led him out onto the aisle. He dragged fresh straw out onto the clean floor. She grabbed the rope cross-ties and fastened them to the rings on each side of his halter. I stroked Diamond Jack's neck. Ingrid brought the wooden grooming box and put it on the floor.

"Let's get a soda," Allison said. She was already a few steps in front of us.

I gave Diamond Jack another pat before I headed to the clubroom.

Allison was lucky. She had her own horse.

I sighed.

"You okay?" Ingrid asked.

"Sure," I said. "Just thirsty, I guess."

As we were about to go into the clubroom, Stan popped out of his office.

"Hi, Stan," we all said at the same time.

"Hi, girls," Stan said. "Cassie, can I see you for a minute? I'd hoped you'd come today."

I followed him into his office. It was decorated with faded blue carpeting, photos of champion hunters and jumpers that hung on the walls, a narrow glass case displaying shelves of tarnished trophies, and one wall totally covered in faded show ribbons. The pungent smell of horses, mildew, and boot polish filled the room. An oscillating fan whirled on top of a low bookcase that shelved a collection of horse books. On the messy desk, the corners of a stack of papers, weighed down with a horseshoe, fluttered when the fan's air passed over them. Stan smiled at me.

"Quite a day we had yesterday, don't you think?" He flipped the pages of the horse magazine he was looking at.

I looked down at the toes of my brown paddock boots.

I wished he hadn't said that. I wanted to forget the whole thing.

"Do you have time today to straighten up the school horses' tack room and clean their bridles?"

I shifted from my right foot to my left one. Normally, I liked to help around the stable. I came for my regular riding lessons on Saturday mornings during the school year and added an extra lesson during the week in the summer. And sometimes I got to ride the nicer show horses in exchange for cleaning tack or grooming the boarders' horses, or picking out stalls. I liked to be at the barn as much as possible, but not today.

"Um ... sure ... I guess." I picked at an old scab on my right forearm. "We're just getting a soda. Allison is going to let Ingrid and me ride Diamond Jack later."

"That's nice of her." He closed the magazine and tossed it on a pile of other papers.

I half-smiled and turned to walk out.

"Before you go, will you turn out Over The Top and Miss Scarlet in the left side back pasture?" Stan asked. "Then bring in the gelding that's in the big paddock next to that one. He's been out there since this morning. He goes next to Rumford."

"Sure." I tried to smile back.

I walked out of the office and over to where the extra lead ropes hung. I took two from a hook. I'd get my soda after I finished the tasks Stan had asked me to do.

Allison was rubbing Diamond Jack's coat in circular motions with a black rubber curry comb. Clumps of shedding chestnut-colored hair fell to the floor. Ingrid sipped her soda and swung her right leg. She sat on a gray captain's chair with navy trim near Diamond Jack's stall.

"Where're you going?" Allison asked me. She snapped and popped her gum.

Ingrid stopped swinging her leg.

"Stan asked me to clean the school horses' tack." I wrapped the lead ropes around and around my hand. "But first, I have to turn out Over The Top and Miss Scarlet and bring in a horse from outside."

"When you're done and I've got Diamond Jack warmed up, come and ride with me." Allison threw the curry comb back into the box and picked out a body brush.

"Okay." I ducked under the cross-tie to get the two horses from their stalls.

Over The Top and Miss Scarlet were stabled next to each other, close to Diamond Jack's stall. I opened Over The Top's stall door first and put on his halter. Next, I did Scarlet's. I clipped a lead rope on Over The Top's halter, then one onto Miss Scarlet's, and led both horses out the open back doors. Bob and his crew had finished cleaning the barn by the time I was done talking to Stan, so the tractor wasn't blocking the back doors anymore.

The two horses and I crunched along the gravel driveway to the back pasture. The other horses turned out in the back whinnied to each other. A few songbirds flew among the tree branches. The tractor and spreader drove past the indoor ring on the path back from the manure pile. Over The Top sneezed, then again.

I liked the walk to the five turnout areas behind the barn. The two areas farthest from the barn, the one on the right and the one on the left, were about four acres each and big enough to be called pastures. The three paddock areas in between the two pastures were long and straight and only about one and a half acres each. Shade trees and green grass were in all of the white fenced-in areas. The turned-out horses either grazed peacefully, scratched each other's withers with their teeth, or galloped, bucked, and played.

More whinnying came from the turned-out horses.

A car door slammed in the stable's front parking lot.

I hated to turn out a few of the horses because they'd get so excited to go outside. I learned the hard way to make the horses stand and wait before I'd let them go. Some of the horses would jump back and try to run off before I had a chance to unclip the lead rope. It felt like my arm got ripped out of its socket when they jerked back and pulled against the lead rope before they were free to go. But the two horses I led were too old to misbehave. They walked quietly into the pasture, waited for me to unlatch their leads, and simply started to graze the first chance they got.

I closed the gate behind me. They swished flies and tried to eat in each other's grassy areas.

"Enjoy," I told them as I turned away and went to bring in the horse Stan had asked me to.

"Come here, boy," I called out to a bay horse that was standing at the far end of the paddock. I opened the gate and went inside. He started to walk toward me. I always carried pieces of apples with me—in case I had to bribe the horses to catch them.

The horse got closer.

I reached into my pocket for the piece of apple. My eyes widened and my mouth opened.

The bay horse's wide forehead had a small white star. He had familiar brown eyes.

I dropped the lead ropes and piece of apple.

The horse nickered softly.

Someone, maybe Keith, had removed the masses of burdocks in his black mane and tail. The person had also pulled the bay's mane to the correct length. He'd had a bath. His coat was redder than before—a blood bay. His legs had four black stockings, but no white markings. I couldn't tell that yesterday when we stood in the paddock of muck at the broken-down farm. He was skinny, but had been the healthiest of the four horses.

"Oh, my gosh!"

The bay came and stood beside me. I wrapped my arms around his neck and pressed my forehead against his sun-warmed coat. He gently pushed his nose against my side. I lifted my head and held out my hand for him to sniff. He gently blew warm air from his nostrils across my palm.

How did you get ... Who saved ... What happened to you?

The bay moved his soft lips across my hand.

"Wait, I've got something for you." I bent down and picked up the fallen lead ropes and piece of apple. He took the apple from my hand and made sweet-smelling white froth as he chewed it.

I clicked on the lead and started to walk him back toward the barn. I still couldn't believe he was right here next to me.

Stan leaned against the frame of the open barn door, watching me and the bay. "So, what do you think of our new horse?" Stan asked. He grinned.

9

HORSE WITH A NEW NAME

"YOU GUYS! COME HERE!" I PUT the bay on the set of cross-ties behind Diamond Jack. "I've got something to tell you!"

"What's up?" Allison had Diamond Jack saddled up and ready to ride. She and Ingrid came over to Stan and me.

"This is one of the horses we looked at yesterday, the one I told you about! You know, one of the horses Dad wouldn't buy for me."

"He's kind of skinny." Ingrid didn't touch him. She looked him over by tipping her head first to the right and then to the left. She squinted her eyes. "Is he going to be all right?"

"Hope so," Stan said. "After he receives some decent care, he should come around just fine."

"How ... how did you get him?" I asked. "I thought he was going to be dog ... I don't understand."

"Couldn't let him go," Stan said as he patted the horse's neck. "No, sir, I couldn't. Even though your dad wouldn't buy him for you, I had a feeling to go and get him. Called Roger when we got back. Said I was coming within the hour with the trailer. Told me

I'd better high-tail it over there because the plant truck was already on its way."

"Weren't you afraid he'd sell the horse anyway?" Allison pulled out a piece of carrot from her pocket and gave it to the bay.

"Roger and I go back a long way." Stan ran his hand over the bay's neck. "He might not take care of horses, but he was good on his word. When I got there, the horse was standing by himself in that muddy paddock. The truck had left with the others. He made me pay an extra $100 dollars for him. It's more than he'd get from the plant. Had a bit of a scuffle trying to load him in the two-horse trailer."

"He wouldn't walk in?" I let the bay sniff my palm.

"Nope," Stan said. "Could be he's never ridden in one before. Maybe he had a bad experience with one at some point in his life. Either way, Roger and I finally got him in. Guess the horse decided he'd better get in the trailer, or he'd end up stuck in that dumpy place, or worse."

"What are you going to do with him?" I stroked the horse's neck and shoulder.

"Put some weight on him," Stan said. "Dr. Walsh is coming tomorrow to check him out. The farrier will be here on Tuesday to trim and shoe him. Look at his hooves."

All three of us tipped our heads to see what Stan was showing us.

The hooves were in bad shape. They were too long and needed a trim. There were some small cracks that looked like they could be trimmed off. I hoped he'd be fine.

"It's strange." Stan's forehead creased, which caused his bushy brown eyebrows to almost touch in the middle. "Someone painted his hooves with black polish ... see how it's worn off in spots. People use polish on show horses. He's in no shape to show. Not sure what they were thinking."

"Do you think he jumps?" Ingrid let the bay horse sniff her hand. I thought he was looking for another carrot.

"Don't know," Stan said. "Will have to wait until he's healthier to see. First, I want to know what kind of a horse he is on the flat. Hope he's well trained."

"Maybe Dad will buy him for me now," I said. "He can get a better look at the bay since he isn't standing in that muddy paddock. The horse is nice. He seems to like me." The bay pushed his head over to me. He rubbed up and down on my arm to scratch his left ear.

"Well, even if your dad doesn't buy him for you, he'll make a nice horse for somebody," Stan said. "Got a feeling about him. Can't put my finger on it, but there's something."

"What's his name?" Allison asked.

The bay picked up his head and pricked his ears. Claire and Joe came inside the barn with their horses after the schooling session out on the cross-country course. They talked to each other as they walked down the right aisle to put their horses on cross-ties.

"Cassie, do you want to name him?" Stan scratched the horse's forehead.

"Hmm ... how about Star ... no, Gallant Star ... at least for now." The horse bobbed his head up and down a few times as if to say he liked his new name.

"Gallant Star it is," Stan said. "Was tired of calling him the new horse. By the way, I took some photos of him with my Polaroid camera when I first got him here. Want to keep track of his progress every month."

"Hey, great idea," I said.

Maybe I could borrow the photos later to show Dad how much Gallant Star was improving. Then he could buy him for me.

"We can see how much he's changed ... like the starving mare's pictures I saw in my horse magazine. She was all skin and bones, much worse than Gallant Star, but within a few months, she was back to being healthy." I patted Gallant Star's neck.

"Doesn't take long for a horse to gain weight if it's in a good place," Stan said. "Well, gotta get back to work. Cassie, you can groom him if you want." Stan gave Gallant Star a final pat, turned, and walked down to the other end of the barn aisle to join Claire and Joe.

"Diamond Jack's getting buggy," Allison said. "I better get on him. Coming, Ingrid?" Allison unclipped the cross-ties, removed Diamond Jack's halter that she had put on over his bridle, and walked him out the front door.

Ingrid followed them outside.

I started brushing Gallant Star and then bent over to lift his left front leg so I could clean out his foot with a metal hoof pick.

Footsteps approached me from behind.

"Hi, Cassie."

My face got hot. I tensed up.

Super-great. Lisa.

"So, is this your new horse?" Lisa asked. "Looks a little skinny, like it's ready for the glue factory. Couldn't your dad spend more than $50 dollars on a horse for you?"

"For your information, he isn't my horse ... well, maybe not yet." I put down Gallant Star's hoof and turned around to face her. Her mom must have dropped her off while I turned out Over The Top and Miss Scarlet. "He's Stan's. And yes, Stan rescued him from becoming dog food."

"Oh, how nice," Lisa said sweetly. "If this isn't your horse, then where's yours? Is it turned out?" She walked closer to Gallant Star.

"I ... I didn't get one yesterday." I watched Gallant Star pin his ears and swish his tail back and forth a few times as a warning for her to keep her distance from him. "None of them suited me. Stan's still looking for other horses for me. I'm sure we'll find one soon."

"Get real," Lisa said. "Like your dad can afford to buy you a nice horse."

"He can, too, buy me one!" I made a fist around the hoof pick.

"Keep dreaming." Lisa walked up to Gallant Star. He pulled up his head, laid back his ears, and struck out at her with his teeth.

"Cripes!" Lisa yelled as she barely managed to jump out of the way. "What's wrong with him?" She backed away, her eyes wide open.

"Guess he doesn't like you." I stood next to Gallant Star and stroked his neck. "Look, he's a sweetie with me."

"Keep that beast away from me!" Lisa tossed her long blond braid over her shoulder as she walked to the opposite side where her flashy chestnut was stabled. "I'm going back to where the REAL show horses are."

"Buzz off," I said when Lisa was halfway to her horse's stall. Gallant Star turned his head toward me as much as he could while on the cross-ties. I patted his shoulder.

After I finished grooming Gallant Star and put him in his stall, I went into the school horses' tack room to check out how many bridles Stan wanted me to clean. A chrome bridle hook, draped with a ton of dirty bridles and standing martingales from yesterday's riding lessons, hung from a chain mounted to the ceiling. It would take me at least a half an hour to clean all of the tack. I needed a soda before I started the job.

As I walked to the clubroom where the soda was kept in an old refrigerator, Lisa led her show horse down the barn aisle and outside. She wore tall black boots, cream-colored breeches, and a pale-blue short-sleeved riding shirt. She had tucked her black velvet hunt cap under her left arm. Her saddle, leather girth, and white saddle pad were brand new. She had talked extra loud at school when she told her few friends about her parents buying them for her birthday, making sure Allison, Ingrid, and I had heard her.

All I'd ever gotten for my birthday was an extra riding lesson and a few new books.

I looked down at my grody T-shirt, the too-small tan jodhpurs with the falling-off leather knee patch I wore yesterday, and my scuffed-up paddock boots with their broken laces. I didn't even own a riding helmet. I had to borrow one from the box of extras from the school horses' tack room.

Mom said we could go shopping for new riding clothes soon. When was it soon? Once, just once, why couldn't something rotten happen to Lisa? She always had the best clothes, the best horse, and even the best boyfriend, David. Why did she get everything she wanted? It wasn't fair.

I opened the door to the clubroom and went inside to get an orange soda.

10
A SECRET

"MOM! DAD! GUESS WHAT?" I ran into the kitchen.

"Take off your boots!" Mom took out a stick of butter from the refrigerator. "I just washed the floor."

I stepped back onto the porch and tried to undo the laces as fast as I could. Dexter came to rub against my legs. I bent down, picked him up, and gave him a cat kiss on the top of his head. He squirmed, pushed, jumped down, and raced back to his dish of cat food in the kitchen.

"Where's Dad?" I asked after I dumped my paddock boots in the middle of the porch floor.

"In the living room watching golf." She put a lemon-yellow mixing bowl on the countertop.

"Come on," I said as I grabbed her arm. "I've got something to tell both of you."

I pulled Mom all the way to the living room. Dad napped in his chair. Dexter followed us in, then jumped into Dad's lap.

"What the ... can't anyone take a nap around here?" Dad said. "What's with the cat?" He pushed Dexter aside and picked up a section of the Sunday paper he must have been reading earlier.

"Mom, Dad, you're never going to believe this!" I said. "Dad, remember the bay horse we looked at yesterday? You know, the one that was with those other starving horses?"

"How could I forget?" Dad turned his newspaper page without looking at me.

"Guess what?" I looked at both of them. "Stan went back and saved him!"

"He did?" Mom said. "That's wonderful, Cassie. What about the other horses? Did he rescue them too? Weren't there other horses, Ed?" She looked at him.

"He was too late for them, but he saved Gallant Star. Well, that's what we're going to call him for now." I waited for Dad's reply.

"That's great, Cass." Dad continued to read his paper.

"Now you can buy him for me." I pulled down the edge of the paper. "He looks a lot better. Stan said the vet is coming, and the farrier will be there on Tuesday to trim and put shoes on—"

"I'm not buying him for you." Dad looked directly at me.

My smile fell down. "But Dad—"

"We went through this yesterday, Cassie. I am not going to buy you a sick horse."

"He might not be sick," I argued. "Dr. Walsh is going to look at him and—"

"I said no. I can afford to get you a nice horse, but you keep insisting on this one. Why is he so great?"

"Well, I don't know if he is." I looked down at the hole in my sock where my toe tip pushed out.

Dad picked up his paper again but immediately slapped it back down in his lap. "I had to work hard to make ends meet for this family, and now that I can finally afford to get you a horse and board it and everything else that goes with owning one—something you've been begging me for years, I might add—and now you won't respect my decision about which one you'll get? Stop asking me about that sickly horse. Do I make myself clear?"

"Yes." My throat tightened.

"End of discussion." He picked up the paper.

"But, Ed, really," Mom said. "Couldn't you take a second look? He sounds like a nice horse. Stan did go back for him. That has to count for something."

Dad folded over the top half of the paper and looked at her. "End of discussion." The paper went back up.

Mom sighed, turned to me, and asked, "Is your homework done? I know it's almost the end of the school year, but you still need to finish the work Mrs. Neumann assigns you."

"Most of it." I inspected my grungy fingernails.

Dad rustled the paper when he skipped on to the next page. He cleared his throat.

"You could do it before suppertime." She put her arm around my shoulder and walked with me toward the kitchen. Dexter followed along ahead of us.

"Do you want a snack?" Mom asked.

"I'm not hungry." My stomach flipped around again. We stopped in front of the stairs.

"It'll be all right." Mom smiled at me. "Your dad will find you a nice horse. Just be patient. And whatever you do, don't bring up this other horse again, or at least for a while. You know how he gets—stubborn and proud like his own father."

"Mom?" I asked as I started up the stairs. Dexter was already at the top waiting for me.

"Hmm?" She turned back to me.

"Can I get new riding clothes soon? You said last week we could—"

"Oh, I completely forgot." Mom looked surprised. "I've been so busy trying to pick out new paint and wallpaper for the kitchen. Yes, absolutely. How about one day after school this week? That T-shirt you're wearing is rag-ready, and the jodhpurs you have on are way too short. You could use better paddock boots too."

"Everything I have is too small or worn out." My stomach felt a little better. "I think Allison is tired of lending me one of her riding coats for shows. I need my own."

"I agree," Mom said. "I'd better get dinner started. Finish your homework, and we'll decide what day to go shopping this week."

"Thanks." I turned and took the steps two at a time.

Dexter raced me to my bedroom.

I changed out of my grungy riding clothes and into shorts and another horsey T-shirt. I sat down at my desk. I pulled out my math book and note papers from the pile of homework I had from school last Friday. A chapter of long division problems waited for me. I loved making the rows of numbers and showing my work.

I tried to concentrate, but imagined what Gallant Star would look like once he was healthy again.

What if Dad saw Gallant Star when he was fit? Dad would definitely agree Gallant Star was the best horse for me. He'd apologize for being so mean and rotten to me, and give Stan a check right away so no one else could buy him. I would ride Gallant Star and show him and win and ...

Dexter startled me by jumping into my lap and then onto the desk. He spread the math papers all over the top. He lay down on top of the mess.

"Hey, I can't do my homework." I rubbed Dexter for a few minutes behind his ears. He squinted and purred like crazy.

"Okay, get down. I have to get this done." I gave him a gentle push.

Dexter jumped to the floor and sprang up onto one of the twin beds. He curled up next to the pillows and promptly started to clean his fur. He'd stop and look at me occasionally, checking to make sure I wouldn't leave the room without him.

I straightened the math papers and went back to the problems. I still couldn't concentrate. I chewed on the cap of my ballpoint pen. The events of the whole weekend ran through my head.

I put the pen down and opened the middle drawer of the desk. I reached in toward the back and pulled out a set of small keys. After I closed the drawer, I used the biggest key to unlock the bottom desk drawer. I pulled out a dictionary-sized carved wooden box Grandma Leona had given me for my tenth birthday, a gift from one of her trips to Europe, and placed it on the desktop. The box opened with the smallest key on the ring.

Inside the box was a pile of private treasures that only I had access to: a mood ring that was always black and never worked right, a blue ribbon I had won in sixth grade for my science project, a charm bracelet with horsey charms on it from Ingrid, a note from Allison she had passed to me during an English class, a purple rabbit's foot I had won at the county fair, and other special stuff I found the need to hang on to.

I removed my most prized items from the top of the stash—Valentines from David given to me in fifth, sixth, and seventh grades. Each card was the same one. They had a cowgirl riding a rearing Palomino horse. The cowgirl twirled a rope shaped like a heart with the words "Be Mine" written inside the lasso loops. My classmates always exchanged cards on Valentine's Day. Everyone got one. It's not like the ones from David were special or anything. At least he knew I liked horses. I only kept his cards and no one else's.

I took out our seventh grade class photo that I had stashed in there. My picture looked super-dorky. My smile was all lopsided and weird. I made a face at it.

Lisa's pretty picture grinned at me. I put the class photo on top of my math homework. I picked up my ballpoint pen and drew inky-blue buck teeth over Lisa's mouth, adding curly piggy-tails all over the top of her head.

"Take that!" I said to her picture.

David's photo was in the upper right-hand corner. His sandy-brown hair was parted on the side. He had a dreamy face with blue eyes and a nice smile. I took the pen and drew a fancy heart around it.

"Why do you like Lisa?" I asked his picture.

No answer.

I looked at Lisa's picture again and made a mean face. My pen tip drew a fat inky X over her whole face.

"That's more like it!"

I paused when I heard Mom talking to Dad at the bottom of the stairs. Footsteps started up the steps. I scrambled to put everything back into the box and shoved it into the desk drawer. I pushed the papers around on the desk and pretended to be doing my homework.

"Are you about done?" Mom asked me from the bedroom doorway. She had an armful of folded towels in her arms. "Dinner will be ready in about twenty minutes. Will you set the table?"

"Sure, I've only got a few problems left," I lied.

She walked to the bathroom, put the towels away, and went back downstairs.

When Mom was gone, I locked up my treasures and put the keys back in their hiding place. I'd finish the math homework later. It wouldn't take me long if I actually paid attention to it.

"Are you staying here or coming with me?" I asked Dexter.

He jumped off the bed and followed me downstairs.

11
THE RIDING LESSON

RAIN RATTLED ON THE METAL roof of the indoor arena. The overhead fluorescents lit up the ring against the dreary gray afternoon. The humid air made the odor of the oiled ring dirt stronger. I adjusted my laced reins as I waited for my turn to jump Old-George-The -Wonder-School-Horse in our riding lesson. It was the middle of June, and I still didn't have a horse.

I dropped my stirrup irons and wiggled my feet back and forth. I wished the circulation would go back into my toes. The stiff leather of my new tall boots made my feet numb. I had blisters too. I couldn't keep my heels down, and I had a hard time keeping my legs in their proper place because the new boots were slippery. They looked great, but I sure couldn't wait to have Ingrid help me pull them off after our lesson so I could put on my old paddock boots. At least my old paddock boots didn't require Band-aids pasted onto both heels and stacked three-high.

"Okay, Ingrid," said Claire. "Your turn. Make sure to keep Bailey in the corners. Don't let him cut inside like he does."

Ingrid was three riders ahead of me. Normally there were six riders in our lesson, but Allison had a dentist appointment and would join us at the barn when she was done, and Lisa never showed up. That was weird. She never missed a chance to rub my face in how super-great she and her horse were. The four of us in the lesson waited in single file to jump the 2-foot, 3-inch-high fence Claire had set up for us.

I watched Ingrid press Bailey into a choppy canter as she made a wide arc into the first corner of the indoor ring. Bailey went along fine until he approached the second corner. He refused to listen to Ingrid's riding cues and cut the corner short. Ingrid tried to pull him toward the red-and-white pole fence, but Bailey slowed to a trot and then veered away from it.

"Don't let him do that, Ingrid," Claire said. "Turn him back toward the rail and make him CANTER into that corner. Show him who's boss."

"I'm trying to, but he won't listen to me," Ingrid said with flushed cheeks.

"Sit up, and don't drop your hands. Keep him moving FORWARD. You've been doing this long enough to know better than to let him take you where HE wants to go."

Ingrid kicked Bailey into a canter, sat upright on him, and came back around the second corner. Bailey looked like he was listening to her, but only for a few strides. Within a few feet of the jump, no matter what Ingrid did, Bailey again slowed down to a trot and barely stepped over the jump.

I laughed.

"It's not funny!" Ingrid shot at me.

It was too funny.

Ingrid rode up behind me and hardly made any effort to pull Bailey to a stop. She made a face at me.

"Sorry, I didn't mean to make you mad," I said.

Ingrid stared at me with flushed cheeks.

I faced forward and waited for my turn. The saddle leather squeaked when George shifted his weight under me. He chewed on his bit.

"Okay, Cassie, ride George firmly, and don't let him do to you what Bailey did to Ingrid," Claire said to me after the other two riders ahead of me had completed their jumps.

I put my feet back into the stirrup irons. I tried to push the weight down through my legs and into my heels, but the boots barely cooperated. I pressed George into a canter and went smoothly around the two corners of the ring. As soon as I headed toward the fence, I felt George slowing down.

"Make him go forward," Claire said. "Use your legs to keep him coming straight at the fence. Don't let him cut out on you."

I tried to keep him going, but I couldn't feel my lower legs because of the boots. George did what he always did to me—he ducked away from the fence and almost unseated me. I grabbed onto his mane to keep from falling off.

"Cassie, you know better than to let him do that," Claire said. She threw her arms up in the air. "Do it again, except this time act like you actually want to JUMP the fence."

"But my boots are tight and slippery. I can't feel my feet."

"Don't make excuses," Claire said. "Use your seat and upper body as well as your legs. New boots are supposed to be tight. Now, ride the fence again."

I adjusted myself in the saddle, gathered up my reins, and turned George around to try again. This time, I was determined to get him over the fence. I rode around the corner and pressed him with my inside leg the best I could. He actually went into the corner! I came around and headed him toward the jump. I sat up, used my seat, and pressed with my lower legs. George was only a few strides from the fence when he suddenly slowed down to a trot and barely made a half-hearted effort to actually go over the fence. At least he didn't trip going over it, and I didn't fall off.

"Hmm, better in the corners, but not so great over the jump," Claire said. "That's enough for today. Cool down your horses. Clean them up, and put them in their stalls when you're done. Cassie, Stan wants me to ride Gallant Star. Do you want to watch? He has been here for almost four weeks now and is recovering nicely. It's time to see what he's like under saddle."

"Sure!" I wondered when they would finally ride him.

"Finish up with George, and I'll wait for you before I get on." Claire walked out of the indoor ring to find Stan and have Gallant Star groomed and saddled for her.

Ingrid and I dismounted from our horses at the same time. It felt like two hundred needles stabbed my feet when I landed on the ground when the blood finally rushed back to my toes. We loosened our girths and pulled the reins over our horses' heads. I limped over the loose ring dirt and wished my feet weren't so sore.

"I bet I could ride a lot better if Gallant Star was my horse," I said. "George is such a spaz. I can't believe he's a retired show horse. Who'd have ridden him if he doesn't like to jump?"

"Bailey is worse than George," Ingrid said. "I hate riding him. I'm going to ask Claire if I can ride a different school horse. I thought you said Stan had a new horse for you to buy."

"He does, but I'm still waiting. He has a mare coming from a show barn near St. Paul, Minnesota. There were some problems with the stable's truck, I guess. She was supposed to be here a week ago."

I wished Dad had changed his mind about owning Gallant Star. I wouldn't have to wait for anything since he was already in the barn.

"Maybe she'll work out for you," Ingrid said. "Let's hurry up. I also want to watch Claire ride Gallant Star."

"The mare might be a nice horse for me," I hobbled along the barn aisle, "I can't hurry up—my feet hurt! Please help me get these boots off."

"I should make you take them off yourself," Ingrid said, "You know, for laughing at me."

"I said I was sorry." I took off my riding helmet and hung it on a hook by the cross-ties.

"No, you didn't," Ingrid said.

"Yes, I did, but if it will make you feel better then okay, I'm sorry for laughing at you. Please, please, please help me get these boots off!" I wasn't even sure we could get them off at all.

"Fine, but promise me you won't laugh at me and make me mad again," Ingrid said.

"Promise," I said.

"Cross your heart and hope to die?" Ingrid said.

"Sure."

"Say it." Ingrid leaned in toward me.

"Cross my heart and hope to die." I crossed my hand over my chest and held up my right palm.

"Good," Ingrid said. "Friends aren't supposed to be mad at each other. Here, let me help pull off your boots, then we can finish cleaning up the school horses."

After I fixed my boot problem, we rubbed the horses down and put away their tack. By the time

Ingrid and I went to get a soda from the clubroom, Keith had finished tacking up Gallant Star and was leading him into the indoor ring. We followed along.

Stan and Claire stood by one of the brightly painted jumps and waited while Keith tightened the girth, pulled down the stirrup irons for Claire, and pulled the reins over Gallant Star's head.

Gallant Star stood quietly while he waited for Keith to finish getting him ready. He looked a lot better since Stan had first brought him to the Oak Lane Stable. His blood-red coat was polished to a sheen, and his black mane and tail were combed out smoothly. His white star poked out from under his black forelock. I wanted to go over and give him a pat, but I knew I had to stand back and just watch.

I wished I was the one getting on to ride him.

"Ready?" Stan asked.

"Let's see what he's made of." Claire gathered up the reins in her left hand and put her right hand on the back of the saddle.

I held my breath as Stan gave her a leg up.

Claire only put her weight across Gallant Star's back without putting her foot into the stirrup yet. They wanted to see if Gallant Star would bolt because he wasn't used to being ridden, but he stood there quietly and chewed on the snaffle bit. Claire swung her leg over his back, picked up her stirrups, and settled into the saddle's seat. She adjusted her reins and pressed him with her heels. He walked forward.

I let out my breath. I had expected the worst, but Gallant Star behaved perfectly.

"Let's see him trot," Stan said.

Claire shortened her reins a bit and squeezed her lower legs against Gallant Star's sides. He moved off into a rhythmic trot. She posted to his long strides. Gallant Star arched his neck as they went around the ring.

"Wow!" Claire said as she rode around the jumps, "He's smooth. A total Cadillac. I hardly have to do anything on him. He responds beautifully."

"I see that," Stan said. "Ask him to stop, then pick up the canter."

Claire sat deep into the saddle's seat, and Gallant Star stopped promptly. She made a small movement with her upper body and lower leg, and he picked up his canter lead perfectly. They cantered both directions of the ring. Gallant Star even did a flying change of lead in the center of the ring when Claire asked him.

"Someone's put some time into him," Stan said. "Not many horses will do a flying change of lead without a lot of training. He's a decent riding horse. Just for fun, let's see what he'll do with a small fence."

"I was already thinking that." Claire turned Gallant Star toward the ring where the low fences Ingrid and I had jumped earlier in our lesson were still set up. Gallant Star pricked up his ears as they rounded the corner and headed for the jump.

I put my soda can to my mouth and held my breath.

Claire sat upright and guided him to the low fence. Gallant Star was only a few strides away when he suddenly slowed down and barely stepped over the jump, like George or Bailey. Claire turned him around and tried it again. He did the exact same thing.

Stan crossed his arms and looked down at the ring. He brushed his right foot through the dirt and sighed.

"Oh," Ingrid looked at me, "he didn't jump it."

My shoulders dropped. I almost wished I hadn't seen him jump. I took a big gulp of my soda and almost choked on the bubbles.

"Can't expect too much on the first day," Stan said as he held the reins as Claire dismounted. "Did a great job on the flat, though. Maybe we can teach him something about jumping. Cassie, do you want to walk him around to cool him out a bit?"

"You bet I would!" I shoved my soda can toward Ingrid and walked over to Stan. I gathered up the reins. Stan gave me a leg up into the saddle. Gallant Star turned his head toward my left foot and gently sniffed my boot toe. I leaned forward and patted his neck.

"Do you think he'll get better at jumping?" I sat back up in the saddle.

"Can't always tell, but maybe," Stan said. "We can do ground work with him and see how he comes along. Be a shame to have him only be a riding horse instead of one that jumps too. Know it was disappointing to watch him take that fence, but don't give up on him just yet."

"I won't." I asked Gallant Star to move forward. He walked off smoothly.

"Brush him off and put him in his stall when you're through." Stan turned to join Claire. The two of them walked out of the ring.

I couldn't help but smile as I rode around the ring on Gallant Star.

I imagined this moment for weeks! He was the perfect size for me. Maybe Dad would be surprised at how much Gallant Star had changed and would consider buying him for me now.

"You look good on him." Ingrid took a sip from her soda can.

"I do sit nicely on him, like he was made for me. Wow, Claire's saddle is a lot more comfortable than George's old saddle."

"Hey, Allison is here," Ingrid said. "She's waving at us from the clubroom window."

I rode Gallant Star over to Ingrid, who stood in the middle of the ring. I was about to dismount when Allison rushed into the ring, kicking up clumps of ring dirt as she came toward us.

"You guys, I've got something to tell you!" Allison tripped and almost fell down. "You're never going to believe this!"

"What?" Ingrid asked. "Tell us."

"Don't keep us waiting." I slid down from Gallant Star's back, ran up the stirrup irons, and loosened the girth. I patted his neck before I pulled the reins over his head.

"Wait, did you get to ride him?" Allison patted Gallant Star's shoulder.

"No," Ingrid said, "She just cooled him down for Claire. Come on, what's the big news? Let me guess. You were at the dentist, so now you have to have all of your teeth pulled because they're rotten from chewing all that bubble gum."

"Very funny." Allison made a face at Ingrid, then she clasped her hands together. "Are you ready for this?"

"TELL US!" Ingrid and I said together.

"For your information," Allison said, "and through a very reliable source, David split up with Lisa! They're over. Finished. Kaput. See you later alligator with NO after while crocodile. Catch my drift?"

Ingrid and I turned to each other, our eyes wide and mouths open.

I thought my insides would burst.

Ingrid turned back to Allison. "No way.

"Yes, way. It's true." Allison crossed her arms and smiled at us.

"What a bummer for Lisa," I lied.

The only way this day would get even more super-duper-great was if I went home and found out Dad had changed his mind and was going to buy Gallant Star for me.

12

On Cloud Nine

As I rode my bike home from the barn, the breeze barely cooled me off from the warm hazy temperature. The shorter hairs around my face tickled my skin with the breeze. The loose hairs usually bugged me, but I was on Cloud Nine after just hearing the nifty news from Allison. I tried to see if David was around as I pedaled past his house, but I didn't see anyone outside.

Dexter met me on the back porch after I charged into the house and let the screen door slam.

"Don't slam the door!" Mom said from the kitchen.

"Sorry."

Dexter waited for me while I took off my paddock boots. We then ran upstairs to my bedroom to change out of my horse clothes. Dexter wove in and around my legs as I tried to put on my clothes.

"Stop it! You're practically tripping me." I hopped on one foot to keep from stepping on him as I pulled on my shorts.

Dexter flattened both of his ears, swished his tail back and forth, and jumped up onto one of the twin beds. He sat down and furiously licked his front paw.

"Sorry, but you're being a pest." I put on a clean T-shirt.

He gave a huff, turned his back to me, and continued to clean his fur.

"If that's the way you want it, fine."

I went over to my desk and took out my secret box. I unlocked it and pulled out my class photograph. I ran my finger over the dark-blue inky X I had drawn to cross out Lisa's face.

Could my handiwork from a few weeks ago have caused her and David to break up?

"Awe, too bad for you, Lisa," I said to her picture.

How does it feel? I know, what a bummer. Now maybe somebody else can have David as a boyfriend, someone like me.

I stared at David's inky heart-encircled picture and smiled. I twirled around the room on my toes as I held the photo out in front of me like a dance partner. I plopped down on the bed across from the one Dexter was on, crossed my legs, and said to David's picture, "So, who are you going to ask out now? Me? Oh, I'd love to go out with you! You want to go to a movie? *The Apple Dumpling Gang* will be showing at the Hartford theater soon. And pizza afterwards? Pizza's my favorite. I could be ready by—"

"Cassie?" Mom called up from the bottom of the stairs. "What are you doing? I could use some help down here."

"Coming!" I got up and twirled and danced my way back to the desk. I held out the photo for one last look, gave David's picture a quick kiss, and locked away the box with my treasures in it.

"Are you going to pout all day?" I looked at Dexter.

He jumped off the bed, stretched long and slow, and walked over by me. I gave him a good rub around his scruff that loosened a lot of black fur. He purred like crazy.

"Better?"

Dexter squinted up at me.

"Guess so." I wiped off the shed hair on my shorts. "Last one down is a rotten egg."

We raced downstairs.

As always, I lost.

13

SNOWDROPS

DAD FOUND A PARKING SPOT IN front of the barn and turned off his car. I held the stack of magazines on my lap that Stan had loaned me. Allison, Ingrid, and I had finished reading them, so I was returning them. I picked them up, tucked them in my left arm, and opened the car door to get out.

"Ready to take a look at this new horse that Stan brought in?" Dad asked as he climbed out of the driver side and closed the Cutlass' door with a thud.

"Dad, I already saw her. Remember? Claire rode her a few days ago."

"Oh, right. I forgot." Dad walked next to me and put his hand on my shoulder. "Hope this doesn't take too long. We've got to be at my company's Fourth of July picnic by one o'clock." He glanced at his watch.

The humid July air made the magazines stick to my arms. The barn felt slightly cooler than outside when we walked in. A fan about the size of the fireplace in our living room whirled at the end of the aisle to help cool things down. Several horses inside their stalls whinnied to each other. A horse down the aisle kicked the wooden wall of its stall. Bob drove the tractor out of the back barn doors after he and his helpers had finished cleaning the last of the stalls, but the odor of soiled straw bedding still hung in the air.

My stomach flipped around when I saw the horse. The dark dapple-gray mare I was to ride stood on the first set of cross-ties on the show horse side of the barn. She was about the same height as Gallant Star, had a refined confirmation, and a well-bred manner about her. Her snow white tail casually swished at flies while Keith finished grooming her dappled coat.

When I walked over to her, she arched her elegant neck toward me and sniffed my right hand as I held it out for her to smell. Her soft gray muzzle tickled my palm.

"Hi, Pretty Girl." I reached up to touch her cheek. Her hair was satiny-smooth under my hand.

"Her name is Snowdrops," Keith said, "because it looks like snowflakes dropped on her dark gray coat."

"I get it," I said.

"She's good-looking," Dad said. Snowdrops reached out her nose to him. He let her smell his palm too. "I hope she isn't too much horse for you. Stan told me on the phone that she's been a champion Junior hunter. She's won a lot of shows or was always in the ribbons. She looks safe enough."

"Dad, she's probably fine." Snowdrops turned back toward me and sniffed the magazines in my arms. She tried to nuzzle them with her lips, but I moved them out of her reach.

I wished Keith would hurry up so I could ride. I never had a horse brushed and saddled for me before. I had to do it myself before my riding lessons on George or if I got to ride one of the better show horses for Stan. It felt strange.

As Keith placed the pad and saddle on the gray mare's back, Stan and Mrs. O'Mally came out of Stan's office. Mrs. O'Mally's Jack Russell terriers were around her feet. They barked and ran toward Dad and me.

Snowdrops looked down at the dogs and snorted once. She lifted her head up and didn't seem disturbed by them. She let Keith bridle her, then tighten the girth a little more.

"Hush now," Mrs. O'Mally said as the terriers gathered around her feet, "you don't need to make so much noise."

"Hi, Ed, Cassie." Stan stood near Snowdrops' head, adjusted her bridle, and fussed with her forelock. "Are you ready to go, or do you need a minute before we start?"

"I've got the magazines you loaned me." I held them against my chest. "Should I put them in your office?"

"Just put them on the wooden chair next to my desk."

As I walked toward the office, I heard Mrs. O'Mally say, "I hope this horse works out for you and Cassie, Ed. She's a pretty little mare. I watched her go when Claire worked her yesterday. Moves nicely, and jumps as neat as a pin. Has good manners too."

I couldn't hear what Dad said to Mrs. O'Mally after I went inside Stan's office. I put the magazines on the wooden chair next to Stan's desk. Papers were all over the desktop. I wondered how he ever found anything since it was such a mess. I straightened the magazine pile on the chair and noticed the top issue had an article on Sky Rocket. There was a photo of the blood-bay horse with his rider on the front cover. I lifted the magazine to read the caption and take a closer look at the picture.

"Cassie?" Dad said as he poked his head into the office, "We're waiting. We don't have all day."

I put the magazine down. "I was just—"

"We've got to move this along. Picnic? Remember?" He pointed to his watch and motioned for me to follow him.

We joined the others in the aisle. Mrs. O'Mally wished us luck and left the barn through the front stable doors with her terriers close at her feet. Snowdrops was finished being tacked up and led toward the indoor ring. Dad and Keith walked alongside the gray mare while Stan and I followed behind them. I noticed Claire had Gallant Star on a set of cross-ties farther down the barn aisle and groomed him. Her tack hung on a saddle rack near her spot. My eyes widened a bit. I looked over at Stan.

"Might as well show two horses if I've got the chance," Stan said quietly as he leaned in toward me.

I smiled.

Dad would get a chance to see what Gallant Star looked like now! I wanted to try out Snowdrops, but I really wanted to ride Gallant Star instead. Maybe I could get on Gallant Star after Claire was done warming him up and after I'd ridden the gray mare long enough. Dad would see what a perfect horse Gallant Star was for me. Well, minus the jumping problems at the moment. Stan could put in a good word or two for me.

Keith stopped Snowdrops in the middle of the ring, pulled down the stirrup irons, and tightened the girth. I walked over to the mare and patted her dark dappled neck. Her coat was silky. I tried to push a small section of white mane over the top of her neck so it would lay on the other side, but the hair flopped back onto the same side. I took a deep breath, gathered my reins, and was lifted up into the saddle by Keith.

I found my stirrups, shortened my reins, and pressed my legs into Snowdrops' sides. I almost jerked backwards when she stepped immediately into a nice walk. I usually had to dig my heels into George's sides before he would go anywhere. I wasn't used to riding a horse that actually cooperated with me.

"Easy now, Cassie," Stan said. "She's sensitive to even the slightest pressure. You don't need to push her like stubborn old George. Ride her lightly."

I took a couple of deep breaths and relaxed. She felt different under me than George did. Her gait was smooth and rhythmic, more like she glided across the ring instead of stumbling along like George did.

"Ask her to trot," Stan said. "Ask quietly, or she may speed up too much. Soft and quiet."

I shortened my reins a bit and squeezed gently. Snowdrops picked up a nice posting trot. She trotted evenly and actually went into the ring's corners when I asked her.

"Good," Stan said. "Keep her moving along ... that's right ... use the whole ring like we taught you instead of going in circles around the edge."

"How does she feel?" Dad's arms were crossed.

"She's comfortable," I said. "I hardly have to work to post on her."

"That's what you need from a horse," Stan said. "Why exert so much effort when you don't need to? Ask her to canter."

Stan turned toward Dad, and they talked to each other in low voices. I couldn't hear what they were saying. When I looked over at them a few minutes later, Dad's face was red. I wondered if he was hot. My shirt stuck to my back from the warm, humid weather.

I prepared to canter Snowdrops, but even before I moved deeper into my seat and pressed with my outside leg, she picked up her correct lead and cantered along the rail of the ring.

"She's great! I could ride her all day." I never rode a horse like Snowdrops before. I wanted to find something wrong with her, but couldn't. I ran my hand over the top of her silky mane near the saddle's pommel. I actually liked her.

I cantered her around for a little while longer and eventually asked her to stop. I needed to catch my breath. I patted her neck and loosened the reins so she could have her head for a while. I saw Claire was riding Gallant Star at the other end of the ring. Dad watched her a few times, but never for too long.

"Let Snowdrops walk a bit," Stan said. "I'll have you jump her in a moment. I'll lower some of the rails along this line of fences for you." Stan pulled down some of the higher poles, threw them on the ground, and rolled them under the jumps.

I walked Snowdrops between the fences near Dad and Stan so Claire could ride Gallant Star around the whole ring. I pulled back on the reins and stopped by them.

"That's a beautiful horse Claire is riding." Dad watched Claire canter Gallant Star, who looked super-good. His red coat gleamed under the lights, his neck arched perfectly, and his black tail streamed out behind him like a flag.

I sat up in my saddle when Dad started asking questions about Gallant Star.

"Believe it or not," Stan said, "that's the bay we looked at on Saturday a few weeks ago. Remember that run-down farm we were at, where the horses were standing in that filthy paddock? I said he might make—"

"That's the same horse?" Dad asked, shaking his head. "No way. This horse looks good. That other one, well, didn't."

"That's what good care can do," Stan said. "Worked wonders on him. He wasn't as bad off as the other three. Came along just fine."

"Dad, I told you Gallant Star looked better than when we first saw him. He's trained well too."

I hoped Claire wouldn't try to jump Gallant Star, or Dad definitely wouldn't buy him for me then if he saw Gallant Star barely walk over a low fence.

"What are you going to do with him?" Dad's eyes narrowed.

"Keep working with him," Stan said. "He needs more time jumping. Probably sell him eventually."

Claire halted Gallant Star, then rode him around on a long rein at the other end of the ring. She dismounted and led Gallant Star out of the arena.

"Okay, Cassie," Stan said as he turned back toward me, "ready when you are. Trot the line first. I want to see how you manage Snowdrops' jumping style."

I had almost forgotten about Snowdrops!

I shortened up my reins, adjusted my seat, and picked up a working trot. Snowdrops and I came out of the corner and headed straight for the line of 2-foot, 6-inch high fences. She never hesitated. She moved forward and took the colorful jumps with grace that I never had with George.

"Oh, my gosh!" I patted Snowdrop's neck after I pulled her up. "She actually jumped the fences!"

Stan laughed and then smiled. "She'd better jump them. She's a good show horse. Let me put the rails up a bit and then go ahead and canter this time. Looks like you've got a good feel for her."

Dad watched me ride.

After Stan raised the fences, I asked Snowdrops to pick up her left canter lead. We again rode out of the corner and came straight toward the center of the line of fences. She moved smoothly and jumped the slightly higher fences with a little more bounce to her gait. It was almost like flying. I had to hang onto her mane by the last fence because her jumping form was nicely rounded over the top of the fence instead of being such a flat jumper like George. I lost my left stirrup iron, but at least I didn't fall off.

"You'd get used to her after some practice," Stan said. "She's got a lot more umph than old George. She's got the best jumping style I've seen in a long time. Be hard to beat at hunter shows."

"She's great!" I was breathing hard from trying to stay on over the fences. "Dad, did you see how nicely she jumped?"

Dad came near me and patted Snowdrops' damp neck. He smiled up at me. "She's a nice horse. Stan, why don't we go talk in your office."

"Go ahead and cool her down a bit, Cassie," Stan said. "I'll have Keith come and get her shortly."

"You don't want me to put her away?" I reached down and ran my hand along her mane.

"Not today. Consider it a special treat." Stan turned toward Dad, and they walked out of the ring.

I practically floated on top of Snowdrops. I knew I had my own horse.

If it wasn't going to be Snowdrops, then I knew it would have to be Gallant Star. Dad was interested in him, too, because Dad had asked all of those questions about him and couldn't keep his eyes off of Claire and Gallant Star when they were in the ring.

I sang softly to myself, "I get a new horse. I get a new horse. I get a new horse."

Snowdrops twitched her ears toward me as I sang out loud.

Keith came for Snowdrops after I took a few turns around the ring. He held her reins while I dismounted and tried to get the circulation back into my feet because my new boots were still giving me problems. I walked alongside Keith as he led Snowdrops out of the ring.

"Did you like her?" Keith asked. "She seems like a good horse. Easy to handle."

"She was great! She has smooth gaits instead of choppy ones like George's." I reached over to run my hand over Snowdrops' shoulder as we walked out.

He smiled, laughed, and then said, "Old George is getting tired and grumpy for riding lessons. Maybe it's time to retire him out to the big pasture in the back where all of the old school and show horses stay for the rest of their lives."

"I'm sure he'd like that. Then I wouldn't have to ride him anymore." I still hobbled a bit from my new boots.

"Looks like you might get your own horse anyway. Good luck." He and Snowdrop headed for the show horse side of the barn.

I had just walked inside the barn aisle when Lisa came through the open barn doors. I hardly recognized her. Her T-shirt was all baggy, she had shorts on instead of boots and breeches, and she wore grubby tennies. She pushed her messy hair away from her face as she glanced at me, looked down at the floor, and beat a path to her horse's stall.

The door to Stan's office opened and Dad came out. He made that face when he's really mad, but doesn't want anyone to know he's really mad.

"Cassie, we're going," he said. "Now."

"Dad?" I felt glued to the floor.

My stomach flipped around big time.

Stan came out of his office, not smiling. That wasn't like him. "Ed, just think about the offer. I'm sure you'll see it's a fair price."

Dad looked at Stan, turned to me, and said in a louder voice, "Let's go, Cassie. Stan, I'll call you later when you've had some time to reconsider the purchase amount."

"Ed, it's a good price for a good horse." Stan folded his arms across his chest.

Which horse was he talking about? Did I still get one of them?

"Let's go." Dad walked out of the barn.

I raised my hand a bit to Stan and followed after Dad. He had already started the car when I got to the passenger door. I got in, closed the door, and buckled my seatbelt. I sank down in the seat, afraid to ask him anything until he stopped looking so mad.

Dad stared straight ahead and drove on, his hands gripping the steering wheel. After we pulled out of the stable's driveway and headed home, he said more to himself than me, "Stan was asking way too much for the horse. We couldn't agree on the price. Maybe he'll come to his senses and be more reasonable when he's had a chance to think things over."

I wanted to ask him which horse he was talking about, but all I'd do is make him more mad.

I glanced over at him.

"Sorry, Cass. No horse for you today." He turned back to watch the road.

I had already figured that out.

14
GALLANT STAR'S SURPRISE

ALLISON, INGRID, AND I RODE our horses back toward the barn after first riding in the front ring for our lesson with Claire and then outside on the event course to cool down the horses.

"It's getting dark and cloudy," Allison said. Diamond Jack sneezed and almost pulled the loose reins from her hands. She shortened them up when he raised his head back up.

"I heard thunder." Ingrid let Bailey walk next to George's left shoulder.

"I heard it too." I pulled the right rein to make George move away from Bailey and give myself more room. "Let's get inside before it rains."

We walked back to the barn, dismounted in front, and led the horses inside. Our horses' shod hooves clattered on the concrete floor. Someone had turned on the barn's lights because of the darkening sky.

As we came inside, I noticed the indoor ring's gate was closed. Someone must have turned a horse or two in there for them to burn off some steam before they were ridden. I heard dirt occasionally hit the sides of the indoor ring's walls from the churning hooves as the horses raced around inside.

I walked George down to the end cross-tie, Ingrid put Bailey on the one closest to me, and Allison put Diamond Jack on the first cross-tie on the aisle. I grabbed George's halter that hung on the hook by the cross-ties, removed his bridle, and put the halter on him. He tried to scratch against me, but I pushed his head away.

Thunder rumbled outside.

"What are you going to do, Cass?" Allison asked. She stood by me with her saddle and bridle in her arms. "Shady Creek Stable's schooling show is at the end of July. That's only two weeks away. Is your dad going to buy Snowdrops for you, or do you have to ride George?"

"I don't know." I unbuckled the girth and pulled off the saddle. "Dad and Stan can't agree on a price. I guess I'll have to ride George if they don't make some kind of deal soon."

Allison scrunched up her face. "I don't know how you could ride him in a show again. Maybe Claire will let you wear some spurs and carry a crop. He seems to go better then."

"Maybe," I said. "He needs something to keep him going."

"Why don't you ask Stan if you can at least ride Snowdrops in the show?" Ingrid said. "He might let you. You'd do better on her than with George."

"I don't know," I said. The three of us walked into the tack room with our riding gear. "I don't want to seem like Snowdrops is going to be my horse if she's not going to be my horse. I don't understand why this is taking so long." I hung up my bridle and slid the saddle onto its wall-mounted rack. "How hard is it to buy me a horse?"

After we put our stuff away, Allison and Ingrid went back to brush their horses while I walked to the clubroom to get a soda. Thunder grew louder, and the wind had picked up.

The clubroom was lit only by a table light's bright glow. I grabbed a soda from the refrigerator when I heard the horses still running around in the indoor ring. I looked out the big window into the ring and saw only one horse galloping around. The horse bucked and kicked and seemed to have a great time. I thought it was one of the boarders' horses.

As I pulled the tab on my soda can, the horse charged past the window and headed directly toward the jumps. I was about to put the can to my mouth when I saw the strangest thing. Instead of avoiding the jumps, like most horses did, this horse soared over a 3-foot, 6-inch rail fence! The horse then bucked and kicked and headed back around the fences toward the 4-foot, 6-inch wall jump. I held my breath as the horse easily sailed over the fence with room to spare! All of its four feet were tucked up under its belly and its tail stood straight up in the air as it went over the top.

The horse landed and ran off to the center of the ring where it lay down, rolled for a scratch, and then stood up to shake off the ring dirt. The horse faced my direction. Its forelock was pushed to one side. The white star on its forehead stood out.

"Stan!" I almost dropped my soda as I ran for the office. "Stan! You've got to see this!"

I popped into the office and saw Stan sitting at his desk, talking on the phone. He covered the receiver end with his hand and said, "I'm on the phone. Be with you in a minute." He went back to his conversation.

I ran back to the indoor ring and looked over the gate. Gallant Star sniffed and snorted at something on the ground. His head bobbed up when it thundered. He turned when he saw me and trotted over to the gate.

"What's up with you?" Ingrid asked. She and Allison had rushed over to join me.

Gallant Star reached his head over the gate.

"What's wrong?" Allison looked inside the ring.

"Nothing is wrong," I smiled like crazy. "The complete opposite of something is wrong. Something is so right. Gallant Star jumped!"

"This horse actually jumped?" Ingrid squinted at me as Gallant Star pushed his velvet nose into her hand. She let him sniff it. "A real jump? Are you sure you weren't daydreaming in the dark?"

"I saw him jump a 3-foot rail fence and then the 4-foot wall." I rubbed my hand over Gallant Star's cheek to brush off the loose ring dirt. "He ran around the ring and suddenly headed for the jumps all on his own. He cleared them easily. You should have seen him!"

"Cassie, is everything all right?" Stan hurried over to us. "Sorry, I had to take that call. Is something wrong with Gallant Star?"

"Cassie saw Gallant Star jump!" Allison said.

"Jump?" Stan jerked his face toward me.

"I saw him jump a rail fence and then the wall all on his own." My eyes got wide. I talked fast as I pointed to the fences. "At first, he was running around the ring and bucking, and then he started to jump the fences!"

Stan crossed his arms and tapped his right index finger against his lips a few times. He squinted at Gallant Star, who had let Allison scratch his forehead under his forelock. A smile spread slowly across Stan's mouth. "Just jumped on his own? And the bigger fences too?"

"He did," I said. "Why would he jump the 4-foot wall on his own and not the 2-foot fences when Claire tried to jump him?"

"Yes, why?" Ingrid said. "I saw he couldn't jump. He practically stumbled over them, almost as bad as George or Bailey."

"I've got to see this for myself," Stan said as he patted Gallant Star's neck. "But if my hunch is right, we don't have a hunter here, we've got ourselves a jumper. Some jumpers don't like small fences, only the bigger ones. They already know how to do the small ones. It's like making you girls take more lessons on learning the alphabet when you already know how to read. You'd get bored with that, wouldn't you?"

"Really bored," Ingrid said.

"Oh, I get it," I said.

"I'm going to get Claire to school Gallant Star now," Stan said as he flipped on the ring's fluorescent lights. "Cassie, finish up with George, and come and watch if you want to." Stan walked down to the end of the show aisle to talk to Claire.

"I can put George away," I said. "He's cooled off."

"I want to watch," Allison said. "I'm almost finished with Diamond Jack."

"I'm coming," Ingrid said. "All I have to do is brush off Bailey's saddle mark, then I can watch."

After we had put away our horses, Allison, Ingrid, and I headed into the ring to stand next to Stan to watch Gallant Star's schooling. Rain started to hit the metal roof. I hoped Gallant Star would do well. I still had doubts since I remembered the last time they tried to jump him, but maybe this time he would do better.

"Okay, Claire, now that you've got him warmed-up," Stan said, "ride him down to the rail fence. Make sure you sit up on him and keep him moving forward."

"Let's see what this boy is made of," Claire said as she turned him toward the fence.

I was rigid as Gallant Star headed for the bigger fence. I glanced at Stan.

Would he jump it, or would he refuse it like before? My stomach tightened into a knot.

"Keep him steady," Stan said. He never took his eyes off of Claire and Gallant Star. "Looks good."

Gallant Star approached the fence. His ears pricked up and he adjusted his stride. With a big leap, he cleared the fence with room to spare and landed safely on the other side. Claire gave him a pat on the shoulder before pulling him up at the other end of the ring. All of us let out our breath.

"Let's see what he can really do," Stan said. "Ride him along the far side of the course. Do maybe three or four fences in a row. I want to see how consistent he is with more than one fence to jump. If you feel like you're getting into trouble, pull him up, or circle him around the ring."

Claire cantered Gallant Star across the ring and headed him toward the line of 3-foot to 4-foot high fences. I clasped my hands together and watched the approach. Like the last fence, Gallant Star jumped all of them clean and even gave a little buck after the last fence.

"He did it!" I grabbed Ingrid's and Allison's arms and hopped in place. "He did it! I knew he could do it!"

"I wouldn't have believed it unless I saw it myself," Ingrid said. "I guess he can jump."

"He did super-great," Allison said. "You're hurting my arm."

"Oh, sorry," I said as I let go of her. I felt like jumping around the ring myself.

Claire rode Gallant Star over to where we were standing, pulled him up, and ran her hand over the top of his neck. "Nice horse. See, he needed someone to have some faith in what he could do."

Stan was quiet. He patted Gallant Star's neck.

Lightning lit up the sky. Thunder rumbled as rain poured down in buckets onto the roof.

"Did he do something wrong?" I asked.

Stan turned to look at me. "No ... there's just something. Can't put my finger on it ... just ... something."

Claire dismounted, pulled up her stirrup irons, loosened the girth, and headed out the ring leading Gallant Star. Stan walked next to her, and the two of them discussed future training sessions for Gallant Star. Allison, Ingrid, and I tagged along.

"What time is it?" Ingrid asked.

Allison looked at her Mickey Mouse watch. "It's almost three."

"I have to meet Mom soon by the front barn door." Ingrid's cheeks got all rosy-pink. "She's picking me up to go shopping. I need something to new wear. I have a date."

"What?" I hardly heard her last words because she talked so quietly, and it thundered again.

Her face turned red. "I have a date."

"A date?" Allison said after she popped a bubble. "With who? You never told us you liked anyone."

"Yeah, with who?" I asked.

"David," Ingrid said. "Oh, Mom's here. See you later alligators." She ran out to the car that had pulled up near the barn's open doorway. The car's wipers swiped off the rain as fast as it poured onto the windshield. The car backed away, and drove off.

Had I heard her right?

"David?" Allison said. "Wow, she's not going to make any Brownie points with Lisa, that's for sure. You okay?"

I couldn't move. My cheeks felt hot. "I ... I'm just surprised she's going on a date." My arms and thighs jingled with tiny twitches. My breathing stopped, but my heart raced a mile a minute. My temples throbbed.

"I know, neato. Hey, since Ingrid is going out, do you want to sleepover tonight? We can watch the Partridge Family and then maybe a movie if—"

"Sorry, I ... I can't." I played with my long braid as I stared out the barn door. "Grandma Leona is coming over ... for dinner. I haven't seen her since she got back ... from New York. Maybe another time. I'd better call Mom ... see if she can pick me up since it's pouring like crazy ..."

I turned slowly and left Allison standing by the barn's doorway, staring at me while she chewed her gum. I walked like a zombie to the office to call home. I barely remembered my number when I dialed the phone.

15

MISERY LOVES SCISSORS

IT WAS STILL RAINING, BUT NOT AS hard as it had been at the stable. Water dripped off the edge of the roof outside my bedroom window. I sat cross-legged on one of my beds. Dexter was curled up in my lap. I had gotten soaked running to the car from the barn when Mom picked me up and then when I ran into the house when we got home. The wet clothes I had changed out of were still on the floor in a soggy mess. The dark blue towel I had used to dry off my wet hair lay next to me on the twin bed. I think it made the bedspread damp, but I didn't care.

I looked down at Dexter. "Why? Why didn't David ask me out? Is there something wrong with me? Why did he ask out Ingrid?"

Dexter squinted up at me, put his left front paw against my leg, and curled his toes a few times.

"She isn't special or anything." I picked up the towel, rolled it into a ball, and shot it across the floor. "She has braces! Tell me, what boy likes a girl with braces?"

Dexter got dumped out of my lap when I threw the towel. He flattened his ears. He settled down near me with his back toward me and cleaned his fur.

"You're no help," I turned to stare out the window. "What do cats know about boys anyway?"

I got up and went over to my desk. I sat down, pulled out my special box, and unlocked it. David's Valentine cards were on top. I placed them on the desktop. The class photo came out next. I looked over the smiling faces of my classmates, except Lisa's, of course, since her picture had an inked X all over it. Everyone looked happy, except me.

I held the class photo in my left hand. I ran my right hand over it. My fingers clenched and bent the picture as I tried to rip it apart, but the shiny stuff on the front made it too hard to tear up. I grabbed the scissors from the pencil can on my desk and first cut out Lisa's photo. I snipped it up into little bits on top of the desk. Then, I cut out Ingrid's photo.

"Some friend you are!" I shouted as the tiny snips of her photo joined Lisa's pile.

I stopped.

David's picture smiled at me from within the flowery inky heart I had drawn around it. My face felt warm. I tried to swallow, but my throat felt all dry and sore. My nose got all runny.

"Why ... why didn't you ask me out?" My heart beat so hard I could hear it in my ears.

No answer.

I wiped my nose with the back of my hand that held the scissors and carefully cut around the ink heart until David's picture was freed from the rest of the class photograph. I laid it on the desk while I cut up the rest of the class photo. I then picked up David's picture. I gave him one last look before I started to cut up his picture into even smaller pieces.

I put the scissors back into the pencil can and sat back in my chair. The small stack of Valentine cards from David sat on the desk. I leaned forward, picked up the top one, and ripped it into pieces. I did the same with the other two. I added them to the cut-up photos, scooped the pile into my hands, and tossed the whole works into the trash. The pieces looked like New Year's Eve confetti as they fell to the bottom, except I wasn't celebrating anything.

"You ... guys ... stink!" I tried to shout at the trash can, but my throat got all choked up. My face felt all hot. I crossed my arms on the desktop, put my head down on them, and cried like a baby.

16

RIDING GALLANT STAR

THE RAIN HAD STOPPED BY THE time I decided to ride my bike to the barn the next morning. It was still gray and gloomy outside. A heavy-duty cool breeze tousled my long ponytail. A few crows cawed to each other as they flew across the sky above me, soaring with the wind. I pulled out of our driveway and headed toward the stable.

It was a good thing I'd put on my favorite purple sweatshirt, or I probably would've been cold. The sleeves seemed shorter than the last time I had it on. My wrists and lower arms were exposed when I leaned forward to grip the ram handlebars on my bike. I tried to pull the sleeves down, but they kept creeping up my arms, so I ignored them and rode on. I avoided the puddles. I wore my too-small jodhpurs that I'd dug out of the back of my closet, plus the beat-up pair of paddock boots with holes in their soles that would take on water if I splashed through the puddles.

Every time I passed under trees with branches that crossed over the road, the wind would shake off the leftover raindrops and spray them down over the top of my head, making me feel even worse.

I pedaled super-fast when I got to Allison and David's subdivision. The wind must have stung my eyes when I rode by because I had to use the cuff of my sweatshirt to wipe away the tears. I tried to look straight ahead when I passed David's house, but I slowed down when I saw a moving van with guys unloading furniture in the driveway by the house next to his. Allison hadn't said anything to me about new people moving into her neighborhood.

Once I rode past the subdivision, I slowed down. A herd of black and white Holstein cows grazed in their field near the roadside.

"Boys are dumbheads," I shouted out to the cows.

They looked up at me briefly and returned to their wet grassy breakfast.

I coasted by the small hobby farm that was on my right just before I got to Oak Lane Stable's driveway. I looked for the three horses that were usually outside in their pasture, but didn't see any of them. They must have been kept inside their barn because of the thunderstorms we'd had over night.

I turned into Oak Lane Stable and pedaled down the long drive. Several horses had been turned out in the white fenced-in pasture along the driveway. They all had a good roll because their bodies were plastered with mud. All of their manes and tails blew around like crazy in the wind. They kept their noses to the ground to graze.

When I was almost to the barn, I saw Allison's bike parked outside. I also noticed several of the rail jump stands in the front ring had blown down in the storm. I parked my bike next to Allison's and was about to walk over to the ring to fix the jumps when Mrs. Wagner came out of the barn leading her pudgy dappled- gray mare. I could already tell she was going to need some help getting on her horse. The gray mare pranced and snorted at everything.

"Need some help?" I asked as I walked up to them.

"Oh, Cassie, you're such a dear to always give me a hand with her," Mrs. Wagner said. "I think it's too windy for her. She's being silly, of course." She tried to get her gray mare to stand by the mounting block, but the horse had other ideas, like going back into the barn.

"Here, let me take the reins." I grabbed them and put my right hand on the mare's neck to try and settle her down. "I think you can get on now."

Mrs. Wagner stepped up onto the mounting block, took the reins in her left hand, and swung up. She sat down in the saddle with a quick plop. The gray mare stepped off almost before Mrs. Wagner could get her feet in the stirrup irons.

"Thanks, Cassie." Mrs. Wagner kicked her round gray mare toward the front ring. I followed along behind them. Her mare danced sideways the whole way there.

Why didn't she just ride inside?

I walked into the ring and picked up the tipped over jump stands and rails. I avoided any puddles since my left paddock boot had a hole in it. My sock was getting damp. Mrs. Wagner's mare skittered away from a bouquet of white plastic daisies that had blown out of the flower box jump in the night. I grabbed them and pushed them back into the box alongside the others.

"Have fun," I said, although I didn't think she'd ride too long.

Mrs. Wagner nodded at me. Her mare was being impossible. She shied away from something else in the ring. Mrs. Wagner needed to take control. I hoped she wouldn't get dumped off. I didn't feel like chasing a loose horse.

The warm horsey smell met me inside the barn. Most of the big doors were closed because of the strong, cool wind. Allison had Diamond Jack on crossties. She tossed a brush into her grooming box and patted his long neck.

"Hi." I let Diamond Jack sniff my left palm while I stroked his cheek.

Allison looked me over, popped a pink bubble, and asked, "Are you riding today?"

"Maybe. Why?"

Allison looked me up and down. She blew a bubble.

I looked down at my clothes.

"Nothing." She picked up her grooming box and headed for the tack room. "I just thought you'd wear your boots and breeches, that's all."

I should have worn my new riding clothes. Why did I wear these old ratty things?

Allison came back from the tack room, carrying her saddle, pad, girth, and bridle. She placed them on the saddle rack in the aisle. She picked up the white saddle pad and smoothed it over Diamond Jack's back.

I held the cross-tie by his head and kept the pad in place while Allison went to get the saddle.

"Is Ingrid coming today?" Allison asked as she put on the saddle and reached under Diamond Jack's front legs for the girth. "She has to tell us EVERY-THING about her date."

"How should I know?" I looked at Diamond Jack's neck.

"What's wrong with you?" Allison asked after tightening the girth. She popped a pink bubble and stared at me.

"Nothing. I'm just—"

"Hi, girls," Stan approached us from his office. "Cassie, can you help out this morning? I need to get three school horses ready for their class. Claire's running late, and Keith's out with a family issue."

"Sure. Which ones do you need?" I slipped away from Allison and followed Stan down the barn aisle.

"Get George, Bailey, and Nicholas ready. Class starts at 10:30. It's only 9:50. You've got plenty of time to knock the dust off of them and tack them up."

As I opened Nicholas' stall door, Stan went back to his office. Allison took Diamond Jack off of the cross-ties and walked him into the indoor ring to ride. None of the school horses had been turned out in the mud that morning, so the three I had to work with would be pretty easy to brush off and get saddled before the lesson started.

After I had Nicholas on the cross-ties and rubbed his red roan coat with the black rubber curry comb, he jerked his head and pricked up his freckled ears when Mrs. Wagner and her spooked gray mare came back inside the barn, clattering frantic hooves along with the wind slamming the barn door closed.

"Will you settle down!" Mrs. Wagner scolded her horse. It must have taken all of her strength to hold onto the mare.

The dappled-gray mare pulled back against the reins with her head held high. The whites of her eyes showed, and her nostrils flared. She danced around on the concrete aisle, leaving small white scrapes from her iron shoes. Other horses in their stalls started to whinny at all the commotion she was making.

I was about to go and help when Stan came out of his office.

"What's going on ... whoa, girl," Stan said. "Whoa. It's all right." He went over to the pair struggling in the aisle and took the reins from Mrs. Wagner's hands.

"The wind has her all ruffled up," Mrs. Wagner said.

"Easy girl," Stan ran his hand over the mare's shoulder. "You're fine. Nothing is going to hurt you. There, she's settled down now." Stan handed the reins back to Mrs. Wagner.

"She doesn't behave at all when it's windy. She spooks so."

"Just ride her inside, or lunge her in the ring on those days," Stan said. "Don't get into a fight with her."

The pudgy mare stood quietly on the cross-ties while Mrs. Wagner untacked her. Stan ran his hand under the mane and along the gray's neck a few times.

"Stan, I wanted to ask you something," Mrs. Wagner said. "Do you have a few minutes?"

"Sure, but not too long," He gave the mare a final pat on her shoulder, "I have to start a lesson for Claire."

The two of them left the dappled-gray mare standing on the cross-ties while they went into Stan's office and closed the door.

I finished grooming Nicholas. I took off my purple sweatshirt and hung it on one of the bridle hooks in the aisle. It was hot work getting the school horses ready. I tacked up Nicholas, put him in his stall, and went to get Bailey. It didn't take me long to have him groomed, saddled up, and ready to go. Then, I grabbed George from his stall and put him on cross-ties.

After I picked out a brush from my grooming box, the office door opened and Mrs. Wagner came out with Stan.

"Let me know what you want to do," Stan said to her.

"I'll call you early this week." Mrs. Wagner walked back over to her gray mare, who stood quietly in the aisle. The mare stretched out her nose toward her owner. Stan walked toward the indoor arena.

Just as I finished brushing George, a car door slammed outside. Someone came inside the barn and pushed hard against the side door to close it because of a wind gust.

Great, Lisa. What was she doing here? She hasn't been around for ages, and now she decides to come today?

Lisa walked down the show horse aisle toward her horse's stall. Her hair was pulled back into a neat long braid, and she was dressed to ride in new-looking clothes.

Why did she suddenly look so good? What happened to her messiness? Great.

I scooted for the tack room to get George's saddle and bridle, but also to hide out in there for a while, or at least until Lisa finished grooming and tacking up her horse. I pulled George's saddle down from its rack and took his bridle off of its hook. I sat down on one of the boarder's tack trunks and waited. I picked at the loose suede knee patch on my too-short jodhpurs. It came off more. I stopped.

"Cassie?" Stan poked his head into the doorway and startled me. "Almost done with the school horses?"

"I have to finish George. Is there something else you want me to do?"

"Would you like to ride Gallant Star? Claire's too busy today. He was in the indoor this morning to get some exercise, but he could use a good ride."

"Sure!" I jumped up off of the trunk. I adjusted George's tack in my arms and practically ran for the doorway. I stopped first, and peeked to see if Lisa was gone yet. She was. I headed over to George and put the tack on the saddle rack.

"Let me know when you have Gallant Star ready to be saddled." Stan started to walk back toward the office. "Want to look at the Polaroids I've taken of him."

"Okay," I said as I put the pad and saddle on George. I tightened the girth, put on his bridle, and led him back into his stall. I put the reins over his neck and looped them behind the run-up stirrup irons so he couldn't put his head down. I patted his neck, closed the stall door, and went to get Gallant Star.

Gallant Star nickered and came over to me when I went into his stall to put on his halter.

"Hi, boy. How are you?" He nuzzled the palm of my left hand while I pressed my right cheek against his neck. His coat felt warm and smooth and smelled super-horsey.

I put him on the cross-ties I'd had George on. I picked out his hooves and started to rub his blood-red coat with a black rubber curry comb. He must have rolled in the ring because the dirt came off of him along with some shedding hair. He pushed against me when I rubbed along the top of his rump. It must have felt good to him.

After I was done, I brushed him with a body brush, combed out his mane and tail, and finished up by wiping a towel across his coat—to make it extra shiny. My T-shirt was pretty grody by the time I was done. I went to get Stan. He was coming out of the indoor.

"Gallant Star is done," I said.

"Let me grab the Polaroids of him. Got them on my desk." Stan ducked into the office and came out with a handful of glossy photos. "Let's see how far he's come since we've had him."

When we stood by Gallant Star, Stan held up the Polaroids he had taken over the past two months. One by one he compared them to Gallant Star's current condition. Stan's eyebrows suddenly creased, almost to where they touched in the middle. He rubbed his left hand over his chin. His eyes darted back and forth from the last photo in his hand to Gallant Star's head. He pushed Gallant Star's forelock out of the way of his star. He squinted closer at the photo.

"What is it?" I asked.

Gallant Star stretched his nose toward Stan.

"Does his star look the same to you, or is it bigger now than when I first bought him? Stan handed me the Polaroid. "Know it's kind of blurry, but what do you think?"

I compared the photo to Gallant Star. He must have wanted to see it, too, because he reached for it with his soft horse lips.

"No, Gallant Star," I said as I pulled it away from him. "I can't really tell. The picture is kinda fuzzy. It sort of looks different."

"Hmm." Stan put the Polaroid I handed back to him in with the rest of the stack he held in his hand. He tapped them against his palm like a deck of playing cards.

"Is something wrong?" I ran my hand over Gallant Star's satiny shoulder.

"Don't think so," Stan said as he put the photos in one hand and gently pulled Gallant Star's forelock back in the center of his forehead. "Just something.

He's looking a lot better then when he first came here, that's for sure."

"He does, doesn't he?" I let Gallant Star nibble my outstretched flat palm with his lips. I closed my eyes for a second and took a deep breath. "Stan?"

He looked straight at me and smiled.

"Could I ... I mean ... if it's all right." I looked down and cleared my scratchy throat. Gallant Star still licked my palm. "The Shady Creek Stable schooling show is two weeks away. Could I ride Gallant Star in it? Only in the flat classes, of course. I couldn't do the Children's Hunt Seat classes with him because he doesn't like to jump so low, and I can't jump as high as he can yet and—"

"Cassie, no." Stan stroked Gallant Star's forehead.

My shoulders slumped. My heart sank into my paddock boots.

"He's quiet enough around here, but a show is a different experience for a horse." Stan scratched Gallant Star behind his left ear where the halter's crown piece rested. "Planned on taking him along. Don't want you or anyone else getting hurt if he gets excited and is hard to control. If he behaves himself, I'll have Joe McLaine show him in a Green Jumper class—see how he handles himself. Claire will be too busy getting you girls ready for your classes to ride him."

"Could I maybe ride Snowdrops then?" I asked. "She's used to horse shows."

"Actually, I thought I'd have you ride her, maybe seal the deal with your dad, but Mrs. Wagner is interested in buying Snowdrops for her daughter. Just asked me today. Said something about wanting them to have matching gray horses to ride together."

My eyes popped. My mouth dropped open.

Mrs. Wagner was going to buy Snowdrops?

"Guess George will have to do." Stan gave Gallant Star a final pat on his nose. "He's not so bad. Perks up at horse shows anyway."

The aisle suddenly filled with voices and a loud banging noise as the three riders who came for their riding lesson tried to close the barn door behind them. Stan went to give them directions. All three of them came down the barn aisle to get their designated school horses and lead them into the indoor ring to mount up.

My face burned when I went to get Gallant Star's saddle and bridle from the show horse's tack room.

What was Dad waiting for? Mrs. Wagner was going to get Snowdrops now. At this rate, I'd never get a horse.

As I walked down the aisle with the saddle and bridle, Allison came out of the indoor leading Diamond Jack. She walked alongside me.

"You're going to ride Gallant Star?" She chewed her pink bubble as she looked at me.

"Yes, Claire's too busy to do it!" I snapped at her.

"Geez, what's wrong with you?" Allison put Diamond Jack on cross-ties, undid his girth, and pulled off his saddle. "You've been a grouch all day. I thought you wanted to ride Gallant Star."

"I do want to ride him." I placed the saddle on Gallant Star's back and tightened the girth to hold it in place. "Sorry. It's been a super-rotten day. I asked Stan if I could ride Gallant Star or Snowdrops in the schooling show, and he said no to both of them. I have to ride George."

"Really?" Allison brushed off Diamond Jack's back to get the sweaty saddle mark off.

"Then I find out Mrs. Wagner is going to buy Snowdrops for her daughter." I took off Gallant Star's halter, gently let him take the snaffle bit, and put the bridle over his ears. I adjusted the leather pieces so they fit him right. "I didn't even know she was married and had a daughter."

Allison stopped brushing midair. "She's married?"

"I guess so, that's what Stan said." I grabbed my purple sweatshirt off of the bridle hook and put it on, although I still felt warm. It would be too cool in the indoor for me to ride in just a T-shirt. Maybe I could pull the bottom down low enough to cover up the top of my jodhpurs.

The barn door banged shut again when someone came in.

"Look on the bright side. Your dad will HAVE to buy you Gallant Star if Snowdrops belongs to Mrs. Wagner." She popped a big pink bubble.

"Hey, I never thought of that!" I tightened the girth a little more. "I like Snowdrops, but I really, really, REALLY want Gallant Star." I patted his side. He turned his head toward me.

"Hi, guys," Ingrid said. She was dressed in a red crocheted sweater vest with pom-pom ties, bell-bottom jeans, tennis shoes, and a floral long-sleeve blouse. "Are you both riding?"

Was Ingrid going to ride in those clothes?

Her face glowed. Her eyelids sparkled with powder-blue eyeshadow. Her cheeks were flushed deep pink. And her peachy-glossed smile was almost as wide as her face.

When did she start wearing makeup?

"Hi, Ingrid. I'm done with Diamond Jack, but Cassie's going to ride Gallant Star," Allison said. "Are you going to ride today?"

"No. I came to see if you guys wanted to come over after lunch. I have so much to tell you about last night. David is so dreamy and so sweet and so nifty."

I get it. You don't need to rub it in.

I turned back to Gallant Star.

"I'll come." Allison unfastened the cross-ties' metal clips on each side of Diamond Jack's halter, let them swing back and clunk against the wooden support posts. She led him toward his stall. "Mom wants me home by lunch, but I can come over later."

"Are you coming?" Ingrid asked me.

"I have to ride Gallant Star, then see what else Stan wants me to help with." I tightened the girth. "I'll probably have a lot to do."

"Oh." Ingrid looked down at the ground.

I took the reins and led Gallant Star toward the indoor arena. "See you."

Allison closed Diamond Jack's stall door. "Have a good ride."

"Yes, have a nice ride," Ingrid said.

"I will." I walked away, leading Gallant Star toward the indoor ring.

"What's wrong with her?" Ingrid asked Allison.

"I don't know. She's been grumpy all day ..."

That was all I heard. I led Gallant Star into the ring.

Once inside the arena opening, I had to let one of the riders in the lesson pass in front of me before I could lead Gallant Star over to the mounting block. Lisa sat on her chestnut horse in the middle of the ring next to Claire, who taught the lesson, and watched the riders trot around the ring. Lisa's reins were long and loopy. Her feet were out of the stirrup irons. Her legs hung down her horse's sides. She barely glanced at me, then looked away.

"Everyone, change directions," Claire said to her three riders. "Make sure to look ahead and cross when you can. Don't get too close to each other. You don't want to cut each other off. Remember to change your diagonals at the center of the ring."

Gallant Star snorted when I mounted him. The wind still rattled against the arena's roof and walls. The noise must have bothered him a bit. He walked off quietly enough. I stayed off of the rail while I warmed him up. I didn't want to get in the way of Claire's students. I avoided Lisa like the plague.

"Halt your horses," Claire said. The regular rhythm of trotting hoof beats came to a stop. "Good. Back them a few steps. John, make sure George backs up in a straight line and not crooked like he's doing. There, that's better."

Lisa picked up her reins, put her feet in her stirrup irons, and nudged her horse forward.

"Walk, and let the horses take a break," Claire said.

The riders relaxed and talked among themselves as they walked their school horses around the ring.

I was about to ask Gallant Star to trot when Lisa cut me off. She pulled in alongside me, leaned in, and said softly, "Pretending he's your horse? And where'd you get that outfit? The Salvation Army?"

"I'm not pretending anything." My cheeks felt hot. My heart pounded against my chest. I squinted at her. "Stan asked me to ride him. Besides, my dad is still deciding if he's going to buy Gallant Star for me." I patted Gallant Star's shoulder.

"Get real." Lisa snorted, turned her chestnut away, and rode over to the middle of the ring. She dismounted and loosened her girth.

"Okay, everyone," Claire said. "Let's pick up the trot again."

I squeezed Gallant Star into a posting trot. I circled around the ring with the other riders, but moved in and out and around the jumps to avoid them. I didn't want to ride only along the rail like they were doing.

Lisa started to lead her horse out of the ring. She had to stop and let the rider on Bailey cross in front of her.

I came out of the corner and pressed a little harder with my lower leg. Gallant Star moved along at a faster clip as I rode straight at her.

Lisa's eyes got wide. Her mouth opened.

I closed my fingers on the right rein and made a smooth turn barely two strides in front of her. I smirked as I rode to the other side of the ring.

Lisa grabbed her reins, pulled on her horse's head, and beat a path toward the ring's door. She disappeared inside the barn.

When I rode past Claire, she gave me the you-know-better-than-that look. "Pay attention to where you are riding," She said to the class. "Always look ahead so you don't cut off the others or almost run them over."

I avoided the other riders in their lesson as I continued to post around the ring.

I imagined what it would've looked like if I really HAD ridden over Lisa. She would've been smashed into the dirt. Her new clothes would've had hoof marks ground into them. She might even have been hurt and wouldn't have been able to ride in the Shady Lane Stable's schooling show. Awe, that would've been a bummer.

I smiled to myself, but made sure I paid extra attention to where the others were riders as I finished up. I didn't want to cut them off and make Claire mad at me.

I finished riding Gallant Star and took him back into the barn.

17

CLEANING OUT THE CLOSET

I NEVER DID GO OVER TO INGRID'S to hear about her dumb date. After I finished riding Gallant Star, I had asked Stan if there was anything else he wanted me to do. He said no, so I rode my bike home. I decided to clean out my closet.

"Dexter, what are you doing?" I knelt on the floor in my bedroom closet, which was a giant mess. I dug around and tried to find my not-so-lucky T-shirt with the ironed-on horse jumping decal. Dexter dove into the mound on the floor next to me and pretended to catch an imaginary something.

"You're a silly cat," I said.

Dexter pushed farther into the pile of clothes.

"There aren't any mice in there."

I went back to my mess. The too-short old jodhpurs with the loose knee patch that I had worn to the barn earlier were the first to go into the pile of discards. I had peeled them off after I got home and left them on the bedroom floor outside of the closet. The old jodhpurs were soon covered up by the un-lucky horse T-shirt, four other T-shirts with horse schlob stains on the fronts that never washed out, a pink sweatshirt with a broken zipper I wore once to the barn, and my only other pair of old jodhpurs with their mud-stained seat, which I had wrecked when I fell off of George last summer while riding on the path by the cross-country course. I thought about throwing out my favorite purple sweatshirt with the shrinking sleeves, but decided against it. The sleeves weren't that short yet.

After I finished making the pile of rejects, I scooped up the heap from the floor and said out loud, "In your face, Lisa. Now say something to me about me and my old clothes." I headed toward the hallway. Dexter rushed downstairs ahead of me.

I took the armful of stuff to the back porch and dropped it onto the floor. I folded the T-shirts and pink sweatshirt and put them into a pile for the rag-bag Mom kept in her sewing room. The too-small jodhpurs, and everything else that was super-ratty, went into a brown paper grocery bag. I'd take the bag out to the garage where the rest of the trash was kept. Dad would eventually burn it in the burning barrel that sat on the far edge of our backyard. I needed to add one more item to the paper bag before I took it out to the garage.

I knelt on the porch floor with the pair of beat-up paddock boots in my hands. Dexter played with one of the many-knotted laces. The paddock boots and now too-small jodhpurs had been birthday gifts from Grandma Leona from a few years ago. I never had new riding clothes before because Mom and Dad couldn't afford to buy me any. It had been the best birthday ever. At the time, the boots and jodhpurs had been a little big.

"Plenty of room to grow into," Grandma Leona had said when she tugged at the waistband of the pair of new jodhpurs I had tried on. She had also pressed her right thumb on top of the stiff new paddock boots to see where my toes wiggled inside. "I don't want you to wear anything that's too tight."

I put the worn-out paddock boots on top of the too-small jodhpurs into the paper bag. I got up and took the bag of stuff out to the garage. I put it next to the other garbage bags ready to be burned. I ran back to the house because it had started raining again.

"Hey, Dad" I flopped down on the couch in the living room, which was next to his upholstered chair. He watched a baseball game. "Guess what?"

He didn't answer me right away. A commercial for insurance came on. Then he answered me, "What?" He yawned.

"Stan told me Mrs. Wagner might be buying Snowdrops for her daughter." I watched his face.

"Well, at least Stan will have a new owner for her." Dad stretched his arms.

"Aren't you interested in buying her anymore?" I asked. "Can't you make a deal with Stan before she does?"

"Cassie, I talked to Stan two weeks ago, and he won't budge on her price. He says it's a fair deal, but I think it's too high. Snowdrops would make you a great horse, but not at the price Stan's asking. Mrs. Wenner—"

"Wagner."

"Sorry, Mrs. Wagner will get a nice horse for her daughter." He went back to the TV.

I picked at an imaginary spot of lint on the sofa's arm. My stomach felt tight. I cleared my throat, "What about Gallant Star? He's still for sale. If Snowdrops belongs to Mrs. Wagner, then couldn't you talk to Stan about buying him for me?"

Dad crossed his arms and stared at the TV. He finally looked at me, shook his head, and said, "No."

"But Stan let me ride him today." I sat up straighter. "Gallant Star went as perfect as can be. He listened to me and everything. Even one of the riders in Claire's class today said I looked good on him."

"Cassie, we've been over this before." Dad never looked away from the TV. "The answer is still no."

I waited a few minutes before saying, "If you need help buying a horse for me, you could ask Grandma Leona. She has lots of money."

Dad shot me a look. His face was awfully red. "I can afford to buy you a horse WITHOUT your grandmother's charity."

"I only thought that—"

"Cassie, for the last time, do I make myself clear on these horse matters?" Dad stared at me.

"Yes." I picked at it some more imaginary lint before I got up and slinked out of the room to go and finish straightening out my bedroom closet.

At this rate, I'd never get a horse.

18

SHOW TIME

THE BREEZE FROM THE OPEN windows of the old stable truck barely cooled me off as we drove the twenty miles from Oak Lane Stable to Shady Creek Stable's schooling show. I stuck my face and right arm out of my truck window to get as much moving air as possible. The last Sunday morning in July was almost ninety degrees by 7:15. I wore my newest pair of beige breeches, a pair of thin knee-hi socks over the breeches' legs so my boots would pull on easier, and a light-blue sleeveless shirt that was pasted to my back from sweat. Mom had pulled my hair into one long braid, but it still felt hot by my neck. The shorter hairs around my face stuck up and out and got all fuzzy from the humidity and the warm breeze. I didn't care. Who'd see me anyway? I'd make sure I tucked the out-of-control hairs into my black velvet riding helmet before I went into the show ring.

"It's a good thing Stan came out of the barn when you tried to load Gallant Star in the two-horse," I said to Keith. He drove the old truck that pulled the two-horse trailer with Bailey and George inside. I had to lean forward to see around Allison, who was squished in between Keith and me. "You didn't know about the trouble Stan had trying to load him after he bought him, did you?"

"No," Keith said. "I knew something was wrong when Gallant Star pulled back on the lead rope and put up a fuss. I wasn't going to force him to get into it. It's way too early and too hot for a fight with a horse."

"I wonder why he's like that." Allison wiggled around to shift her position between us.

"Don't know. Stan's not sure either. Maybe he had a bad experience, or maybe he never rode in a smaller horse trailer before. Gallant Star walked right up the ramp behind Diamond Jack when we loaded him into the big horse van. It's obvious Gallant has traveled in one of those before."

"Maybe he just likes riding in first-class," I said.

"Maybe." Keith reached forward and grabbed his dew-soaked cola can he had perched on the dashboard. He tipped it back and took a swallow. Dew drops fell off the can's surface and spotted his navy blue T-shirt with the gray Oak Lane Stable logo on the front. He leaned forward and put the can back on the dash.

"I need more space." Allison wiggled around again. She snapped her pink bubble gum.

Stan drove in front of us with the stable's six-horse van. He had Gallant Star, Diamond Jack, Lisa's chestnut gelding, Mrs. Wagner's chubby dappled-gray mare, and two other boarders' horses loaded in it. Stan had said Snowdrops wasn't going to the show because she was nearly sold. He didn't want to take a chance on something happening to her. It was only a schooling show for practice anyway. Ingrid rode in the truck's cab with him.

I was glad Ingrid was in the stable's van. I still wasn't talking to her yet because David had asked her out.

Mrs. O'Mally and Claire drove behind us in Mrs. O'Mally's white Chrysler Cordoba. Three other boarders with their own trucks and trailers hauled their horses behind them. Lisa and her parents had gone on to the show before we had even finished loading the horses at the stable.

Figures. Why would Lisa actually help with anything, including her own horse?

"Can you move over?" Allison wiggled around and pushed against me. She blew and popped a huge pink bubble, which came awfully close to my hair.

"Hey, I'm practically hanging out of the truck window right now." I tried to press closer to the door. "There isn't any more room. And don't get gum in my hair!"

"I'm not going to get gum in your hair. Look, I'm boiling here in the middle. You keep hogging the sea—"

"Hey, I know it's a scorcher outside," Keith said as he tried to move over to give Allison some more room, "but we're almost there. It's going to be a long day if the two of you are at each other already."

"Sorry," Allison said. "I hate super-hot days. Shady Creek Stable always has this schooling show when it's, like, a million degrees outside."

"I know," I said. "It's a good thing it's only a one day show." I leaned on the window's ledge and moved my right hand up and down, like waves through the passing air. Shady Creek Stable's sign came into view.

"Show time." Keith slowed the truck down, shifted gears, and followed Stan into the gravel driveway.

Cicadas buzzed in the maple trees that shaded the long curved edge of a shallow creek at the stable's entrance. I watched a robin swoop down from one of the maple branches, land near the water's edge, and take a quick drink before it flew off.

After the long, hot drive, I wouldn't mind splashing some cool water on my face.

We pulled into the driveway. On our right, we passed an old yellow farmhouse decorated with white trim and shutters, built near the road and across from a fenced-in outdoor riding ring where four people lunged their horses before the first classes started at 8:30. Two of the four horses were dark with sweat.

"Why are they working their horses so hard?" Allison asked as she looked around Keith to watch. "I'd never do that to Diamond Jack."

"Their horses might not be as well trained as Diamond Jack. Maybe the grooms need to take the edge off of them before their classes start." Keith watched where Stan was headed.

"Maybe." Allison blew and popped a small pink bubble. "Still, it seems awfully mean to make the horses all sweaty."

I fanned my face with my floppy, crumpled show schedule, trying to cool off, but it didn't help.

The driveway took us past the stable's red brick mansion, which was set off to our right, to the long main barn. The barn had an attached indoor arena where riders, horses, and trainers got ready for the show day. A food vendor truck was parked off to the side of the main barn and already had a short line of people waiting to get something to eat. I was sure I'd be there a ton today—mostly to get something to drink in this heat.

"Mmm, smell that bacon and coffee," Keith said. "I think I'll get something to eat after we're set up and ready to go. The coffee sure smells good, but I'll just get another soda." He tipped his head back and drained the last of his cola. He put the empty can back on the dashboard.

How could he even think about eating? Gross.

"Hey, there's Lisa." Allison pointed her finger in front of my face and out my window.

Lisa and two of her Junior Level riding buddies walked up to get in line at the food truck.

How come she didn't look all hot and miserable?

I knew she saw us, but she turned away when we drove past. She giggled with her friends. Like she was going to help us unload when we parked the trucks.

"Why does Lisa hang out with those girls?" Allison asked.

"Maybe she thinks she's too good for us." I tried to move over a bit. "They're Junior riders, and we're only Children's riders because we're not 14 yet."

"But she's not 14 yet either," Allison wiggled around. "I can't wait to ride Junior Level, then I won't feel like a baby anymore."

"Me too."

I really wanted to ride in bigger A-rated shows with my own horse.

"Hey, Jody," Keith said as he lifted his left hand toward a groom from another stable, who walked near our truck.

Jody smiled and replied by raising up his left hand, which gripped a bucket of bathing tools while his right hand held onto a nylon lead rope. He led a chestnut horse with a white star, a wide blaze that ran down its nose, a braided mane and tail, and rear white socks toward the wash rack. The chestnut's coat was dark with sweat. I could see white sweat lather between its hind legs as Jody walked the horse off to give it a bath.

"I guess Jody's horse also needed the edge taken off of him ... or her," Allison said.

We followed Stan past the left side of the main barn, toward the back. To our left, four paddocks, each with a horse turned out in it, ran along the driveway. Three of the horses ate grass that grew along the fences' edges. The horse in the middle paddock rolled on its back in the dirt, stood up, shook off a huge cloud of dust, and then looked around for some grass to eat. A young blond woman approached the middle paddock gate with a lead rope in her hand. Obviously, she had to clean up her horse again after it had rolled.

We drove behind the main barn to a smaller barn area in the back where we had been stabled at last year's show. It was near a second outdoor riding ring. People milled around the colorful jumps and riding course in the ring that had been set up for the show's jumper classes. Also behind the main barn were four fenced-in pastures—the largest one had lots of horse trailers and the bigger horse vans parked in neat rows.

Stan pulled up in front of the smaller stable. Keith stopped behind him. Stan jumped down from the driver's seat and came toward us.

"Pretty sure we'll be stabled where we were last year." Stan thumped the truck's open window's ledge twice with his right palm. "I'll go check." Stan disappeared inside the main barn.

"Can I get out now?" Allison pushed slightly against me. "I need some cooler air."

"Like you're going to find it outside." I opened the truck door and got out before Allison did. We both pulled at our sweaty riding shirts, hoping to adjust them and make them look nicer. It didn't help. My shirt still stuck to my back.

Stan walked back to us and nodded. "We're in the same stalls. Let's get these horses unloaded."

Stan swung back up into the cab of the horse van and drove it closer to the front of the stable's open doorway. Keith pulled his truck closer in behind Stan's and shut off the engine. Both Stan and Keith got out of their vehicles and moved to the trailers' doors. The other boarders with their own trucks and trailers parked behind us so they could unload their horses.

"I'll park in the pasture." Mrs. O'Mally drove up alongside Stan. "Claire and I'll be right back to help." She slowly drove the long white car toward the big field's parking areas.

Ingrid climbed down from the big van and came over by us. I had almost forgotten about her. Her cheeks were deep pink.

"My face feels hot." Ingrid pressed her hands against both cheeks.

"That's because it IS HOT!" Allison said.

"Cassie, help Keith get George and Bailey out of the trailer," Stan said. "Ingrid and Allison, please help me unload the horses in the van. We'll unload the show trunks once the horses are in their stalls."

Allison and Ingrid walked over to Stan. He pulled out the ramp for the horse van. He attached the ramp's wooden side panels that were used to help guide the horses up and down from the van's interior. The three of them walked up to get the horses.

"Cassie, can you unlatch the other side of the trailer's ramp?" Keith asked me after he had undone the bolt on his side of the trailer.

"Sure." I slid the bolt back. Keith and I lowered the ramp to the ground. George started to step side to side. Bailey was quiet and pushed his nose around in his hay net.

"I always forget how worked up George can get at shows," Keith said. "He sure likes being here."

"I wish he had half the energy he has at shows when I'm having lessons on him. He's so poky at home."

"We all have our quirks," Keith said. "Will you go up front and unfasten his lead so you can back him out once I have his rump safety strap off?"

I walked up to the emergency door at the front of the trailer. Keith had opened it for the horses when he had stopped the truck. I ducked into the trailer through the small side door to back George out. He was dancing around.

"Stop it!" I said. "You'll get all sweaty, and I'll need to wash you off again."

George didn't listen. He whinnied to the other horses.

"Okay, I have his rump strap off. You can back him out now."

I untied the lead rope and stepped in front of George. "Okay, back up, George." He started to move slowly backwards. He felt his way down the ramp and onto the gravel drive. I held his lead rope the whole time. Bailey nickered.

"Hold onto George and undo Bailey's rump strap when I say to," Keith said. "Then I'll grab Bailey's lead and back him out."

I managed to settle George down by the time Keith asked me to undo the rump strap. Keith backed Bailey out and onto the driveway.

"Stan will show us which stalls are theirs," Keith said.

We led the horses into the barn.

Stan had Lisa's flashy chestnut on a lead and walked the gelding into one of the first stalls. He turned her horse around, removed the lead, and closed the stall door.

"You can put George and Bailey next to Mrs. Wagner's gray mare, down at the end," Stan said to Keith and me. "We'll put Gallant Star and Diamond Jack next to Lisa's horse."

Keith and I walked our horses into their stalls, took off the leads, and closed the stall doors.

"I'll get Gallant Star," I said.

Allison walked in with Diamond Jack and asked, "Where should I put him?"

"Put him next to Lisa's gelding," Stan said. "On the right. Cassie will put Gallant Star on his left."

I passed Ingrid, who led one of the boarder's horses from the van, when I went out the stable door. She smiled at me. I looked down and pretended to fix my lead rope's clasp.

"Hey, Gallant," I said as I walked up the van's ramp. "Are you ready for your first show with us?"

Gallant Star nickered to me. He bobbed his head up and down, making the chain ties that held him in place clank against the metal poles that divided the van's stalls. I attached the lead rope to his halter, undid the chain clasps, and walked him down the ramp.

Gallant Star stopped and stood like a statue on the driveway. His eyes widened as he looked at the back ring with its colorful jumps, riders, horses, and trainers walking everywhere. His ears perked up. His nostrils flared. His neck arched. He let out a loud, long whinny. He started to dance around me.

"Whoa! Easy, boy," I walked him around in a small circle. I tried to settle him down by patting his neck. "It's okay. It's only a schooling show."

"Need help?" Stan asked. He had walked up with a lead rope. "Looks like someone else besides George gets excited at shows. I'll take Gallant. Grab the last horse out of the van."

Stan handed me the lead rope, took Gallant Star's lead, and walked him toward the barn. Gallant Star settled down when Stan took him, but he still arched his neck.

"Nice horse you've got there, Stan," said a man wearing a plaid shirt, jeans, a cowboy hat and boots. The man held the hand of a little girl. She had on tiny paddock boots, beige jodhpurs, brown leather gator straps buckled around the tops of her calves, a pink riding shirt, and had two fuzzy braids tied with pink bows near their curly ends. She looked like she might be one of the pony riders. She tipped her head back when she looked up at Stan.

"He's a good one." Stan ran his hand over Gallant Star's neck. "Have him entered in the training jumper class. Want to see what he can do."

"I've got Turn The Tables entered in that class," the cowboy man said. "I guess we'll see who's got the better horse."

"Guess we will." Stan smiled at the man and the little girl. Stan turned and walked Gallant Star up to Claire and Mrs. O'Mally, who were now standing in front of the barn's doorway. All four of them walked inside.

I wished I was riding Gallant Star in the jumping class. How fast could I learn to ride like that if I was going to own and show him? Dad, Mom, and Grandma Leona were coming to watch the show. If Gallant Star won his jumper class, Dad would see how great he's turning out to be. Then he'd have to buy Gallant Star for me.

I turned and went up the ramp to get the last boarders' horse.

"Come on," I said to the dark brown and white Pinto, Scout's Honor, who pawed at the floor with his right front hoof. I undid the clasps to his chains. "Let's get you inside with the rest of the horses." I led him down the ramp and toward the barn.

Keith had pulled out the gray show trunk from the two-horse trailer, put it on a dolly, and was also headed toward the barn. I beat him inside. I put the Pinto in his stall. Keith wheeled the show trunk in and put it next to Lisa's horse's stall.

As we set up our stable area, Stan went to get our show registrations and numbers. Claire and Mrs. O'Mally hung the Oak Lane Stable's gray and dark blue cloth banner above Gallant Star's and Lisa's horse's stalls. Allison, Ingrid, and I filled water buckets. I got sprayed with the hose when I filled George's bucket, but I didn't care. It sort of cooled me off. When I threw in flakes of hay for the horses to eat, the chaff from the hay stuck all over the front of my sweaty riding shirt and right arm. I grabbed a grooming towel to wipe it off. All that did was make a dirty green swoosh across the front of my shirt.

Great. Now my clean shirt is wrecked. Good thing my riding coat will cover it up.

"I need everyone's attention!" Claire waved a piece of paper in the air. "Let's go over the class schedule now so everyone knows what to do. I DON'T want anyone having last minute mad dashes getting to the ring."

All of the riders, including the older boarders, stood around Claire. Thankfully, Ingrid was on the other side of Allison.

Allison popped a pink bubble next to me. She nudged me with her left elbow, leaned in, and whispered, "Nice timing."

Lisa had just walked into the barn and joined us for Claire's pre-show directions. She squeezed in between Mrs. Wagner and Mrs. O'Mally.

Late like always. How come she looked as cool as a cucumber?

"The Ponies, Children's, and Junior riders will be in the front ring," Claire said as she turned to face each of us, "while the Adult Amateur Owners will ride in the indoor. Jumpers will be in the back ring after lunch."

Stan walked in by us. He carried a white Styrofoam cup and a thick manilla packet with the name "Oak Lane Stable" written on the front. He stood next to Keith and sipped his coffee. Keith had gone to get something to eat from the food van after we had finished setting up. He sat on the show trunk eating his English muffin, eggs, and bacon.

How could Keith eat in this heat? Super-gross.

"The Pony riders will go first thing this morning," Claire said. "There aren't a lot of them, so their classes should go quickly. Pay attention to your class order and when you need to get ready. Mrs. O'Mally will help the Amateurs by the indoor, and I'll keep the Children riders going in the front ring. Stan will help out where we need him. Since Gallant Star is our only jumper, and there is only one class since it's a schooling show, Stan and Keith will get him ready when the time comes. Any questions?"

"When do I go?" Mrs. Wagner asked. She always had questions at shows. She wasn't very good with directions even when she was just told them. "Should I start getting my gray mare ready? Where's my number?"

"Got everyone's show number and class registration right here." Stan held up the thick manilla envelope. "Let's hand them out."

"Don't lose them," Claire said.

We crowded around Stan. Stan had Keith get off the show trunk so he could put the stuff from the packet into piles on the top. Stan handed out the registration papers and white cardboard show numbers.

"Let me help you, Stan," Keith said.

Stan handed him a chunk of the numbers from the packet.

"Mrs. Wagner, here are your papers," Stan said, then reaching for another registration and number, "Lisa, here are yours ... Cassie, I saw yours near the top somewhere."

"Allison, I've got yours," Keith said. "Ingrid, here are yours."

After everyone got their numbers and class papers, the adult boarders followed Mrs. O'Mally back to their stabled horses to check out their show order. She was all business when it came to shows. No messing around when she's in charge. She'd keep them on time for their classes.

"Good luck everyone," Mrs. O'Mally said to her group.

19

Ingrid Rides First

"All pony riders to the front ring, and all first-class Amateur Owners to the indoor. The show starts in five minutes," was repeated again and again by a short old man with a gray hand-held megaphone, who walked past the barn door and up and down the driveway.

"Let's watch the ponies," Allison said. "We've got time before our first class."

"Okay," I said. "George seems to have settled down. I don't think I need to wash him off. He better not try and rub out half of his mane's braids like he did at last year's show. He looked horrible." I looked in his stall to make sure he was still eating his hay and behaving. He was.

"Good thing it's only a schooling show," Ingrid said. "I don't think Keith wants to rebraid any horses today. Come on."

"Pay attention to the time," Claire said to us as we left the barn.

Allison, Ingrid, and I made our way through the growing crowd of horses, riders, their trainers, and spectators. First, we went to get a soda from the food van and then up to the front riding ring to watch. I made sure Allison walked between Ingrid and me. We found a spot on the bleachers that was partly shaded by a maple tree. It wasn't that much cooler, but at least we weren't sitting directly in the sunshine. My shirt still stuck to my back. My soda was warm and watery—all of the ice had melted in the cup by the time we got to the ring.

"I count ten ponies at the ring," Allison said after taking a drink from her soda can. "If this is the class, Claire's right, it won't take long before we have to get ready."

We watched the children riders and ponies each take a turn over the barely 2-foot-high hunt course. Most of the ponies did okay, but a few of them didn't jump very well. A white pony bucked his rider off onto the grass. Next, a chestnut pony ducked-out and went around the first jump, then started eating grass in the center of the ring and wouldn't stop. The young rider had to have her mom climb over the fence, grab the pony, and pull hard on the reins to get it to leave the ring.

"They're almost done," Allison said. "They've got their flat class after this. Claire will be mad if we're late."

"First, let's check to see when we go," I said. "They've posted the order on the fence."

We walked over to look at the sheets of white paper stapled to the fence. All of the pages had everyone's jumping order for each of the classes held in the front ring.

"I go fourth!" Ingrid grabbed the top of her hair with both hands "I'll never be ready in time."

"Come on," Allison said. "You'll be fine. I go twelfth. Lisa rides right before you do, Cassie. You don't go until almost the end of the class. Help us get ready. Okay?" She popped a pink bubble.

"Sure," I said.

Sure, I'd help Allison, but Ingrid? I guess I couldn't stay mad at her forever.

"We'd better go before Claire comes looking for us," Allison said.

Too late.

"Let's go, girls!" Claire walked toward us, dodging other trainers, horses, and riders. "Ingrid, why aren't you back at the barn getting ready? I had to have Keith groom and tack up Bailey for you. You need to get him to the warm-up ring now."

"I need to get my boots on," Ingrid said as we rushed back to the barn. "I have to find my coat and helmet." Her face was deep pink. There were beads of sweat on her forehead.

"I've got your gear." Claire reached for Ingrid's stuff. "Pull on your boots and get on. I'll take your coat and show number to the warm-up ring. You can put them on before you go to the front ring."

Keith tightened Bailey's girth outside the barn door before he gave Ingrid a leg up. She gathered up her reins and rode off with Claire and Keith to the warm-up ring where it was already busy with trainers and the first riders of our class. All of the riders took turns warming-up their horses over two jumps that were set to the height of our class. Allison and I tagged along to watch.

"Not too much, Ingrid," Claire said after Ingrid had ridden Bailey around the ring a few times. "Bailey only needs to loosen up a bit. Okay, it's your turn. Come over the rail fence."

Ingrid came around the turn and approached the fence. Bailey sailed over it smoothly. Just like George, he actually moved like an old show horse was supposed to.

How come they're such old putzes at home?

Allison popped a pink bubble and wiped her hand across her forehead.

"Good job, Ingrid." Claire adjusted Ingrid's brown jacket in her arms. "Now jump one more time and that's enough. You need to get to the front ring."

Again, Bailey flew over the fence in mostly perfect form. Ingrid rode over to us when she was done. Claire handed Ingrid her jacket. She put it on and tied her show number around her waist. Keith wiped her boots off so they would be shiny in the ring. He also wiped off Bailey to make sure he looked good too.

"I can't get my gloves on." Ingrid struggled to pull them on. "My hands are all sweaty."

"Here, wipe your hands off on the towel," Keith said. He smiled up at her. "It'll help."

Ingrid managed to pull her black leather gloves on. She made fists a couple of times to stretch them out. She took the towel and wiped off her forehead, handed the towel back to Keith, and let out a huge puff of air.

"Let's go." Claire led the way as we all walked to the front ring.

Ingrid had to wait for another horse to finish before it was her turn in the ring. She wasn't that late anyway.

"Good luck," Allison said.

"Yes, good luck," I said.

"I think I'm going to be sick," Ingrid said.

"Not right now, you're not," Claire said. "You're on deck. When you get inside the ring, keep Bailey moving forward at a nice, steady pace. He knows what to do." She smiled up at Ingrid.

Ingrid entered the ring after the previous horse and rider rode out through the gate. She rode beautifully, and Bailey jumped great. She'd probably get a ribbon. I knew Allison and Diamond Jack would be wonderful and would probably get a ribbon too. Lisa and her push-button show horse would be fabulous. She always got a ribbon.

Maybe George and I would be super-spectacular, maybe even win the class! That would be great for a change.

There was loud whistling and clapping from the bleachers when Ingrid finished riding and left the ring. I bet it was her family.

"Great job!" Claire held Bailey while Ingrid dismounted. "Let's go back to the barn and pull his saddle. There are 20 horses to go yet, but keep his bridle on and be ready to trot him in when the class is done. You had a good enough trip to place somewhere. Allison, let's get you ready."

"I'm going to say hi to Mom and Dad first." Ingrid said as she peeled off her gloves and jacket. She handed them to Claire. She gave her black helmet to Allison. "I saw them sit down on the bleachers before it was my turn. Too bad David didn't see me ride. He's coming after lunch. I'll be really nervous when he gets here. I hope I don't fall off or something. I'll be right back." She smiled wide enough to have sunlight shine off of her silver braces. She handed Claire her reins and raced over to where her parents sat.

David? David's coming? He doesn't even like horses.

My face grew hotter, if that was possible. I ran my hand over my hair and tried to smooth down the frizzles. My stomach flipped around—a lot.

Not great. No, not great at all.

20

ALLISON RIDES SECOND

"YOU OKAY?" ALLISON ASKED ME.

"I need some soda," I said. "Must be the heat. What do you think Lisa will do when she sees David with Ingrid?"

"Oh, she doesn't care anymore," Allison said. She adjusted Ingrid's helmet under her arm. "Didn't you hear? Lisa's going with some new guy. Guess he'll be a freshman in high school this fall." She popped a big pink bubble.

Why does Lisa have all of the luck?

"Keith, put Bailey on the cross-ties," Claire said when we got back to the barn. "Allison, get Diamond Jack out of his stall and groom him. The class will go faster than you think."

Before I helped Allison groom Diamond Jack, I checked on George to make sure he still looked presentable.

George was eating hay. Braids were still in place. Good.

I also said hello to Gallant Star. He nickered and came over to the stall door. He looked at something outside the barn door while he chewed hay. It must have been interesting because he lifted his head up higher and pricked up his ears. He turned around and went back inside his stall to finish eating his hay.

Stan came over by us as we worked on getting Diamond Jack ready for the class.

"How are things going with the boarders?" Claire asked him. She picked up Allison's navy jacket and show number.

"Good enough," Stan said. "Mrs. Wagner's gray mare spooked in the back corner. Always does. Hopes that riding Snowdrops at shows will help her gain more confidence."

I stopped brushing Diamond Jack. I pretended to clean the body brush by running my hand over the bristles a few times. I had forgotten she was buying Snowdrops.

"Okay, Allison," Claire said, "Tack up Diamond Jack, get on, and head for the warm-up ring. Stan, have fun with the boarders."

Stan waved a hand. He walked back to the far end of the barn where the boarders were getting ready. Keith was also helping them out.

Allison put on Diamond Jack's bridle while I saddled him up. I gave her a leg up once we were outside the barn door. She tightened her girth from up in the saddle. We walked over to Claire.

"Just like I told Ingrid," Claire said. She watched Allison trot Diamond Jack among the other horses and riders, "take him around the ring a few times and then come over the fence. He doesn't need to get all heated up."

Allison rode toward the practice fence. Diamond Jack sailed over it in a perfect arc. She cantered around again and took the fence a second time.

"Come back the other way," Claire said.

Allison changed leads in the middle of the ring and came back at the fence the opposite direction. Again, Diamond Jack was great.

"Trot him around a bit more." Claire turned to me. "Cassie, you didn't bring a towel, did you?"

"No, I wasn't sure if Keith was coming with us," I said.

"Please get one. Meet us by the front ring," Claire said. "Allison is about done here."

I went back to the barn, grabbed the towel that lay on the show trunk, wiped off my face, and headed for the front ring. Allison was buttoning her coat when I got there. She tied her show number around her waist. I wiped off her boots and Diamond Jack with the towel while she wiggled her gloves on. Then she picked up her reins and sat popping occasional pink bubbles.

"Allison, gum." Claire held out her hand.

"It relaxes me," Allison said.

Claire looked at her.

Allison rolled her eyes and handed over the pink wad.

Gross.

Claire put the chewed-up gum in a wad of tissue she had pulled out of her jeans' pocket. She tossed it in the trash barrel near the fence. "Okay, you're next," she said to Allison.

"Good luck," I said.

She trotted into the ring. I looked over at the bleachers. Ingrid still sat with her parents. Lisa sat at the other end of the bleachers with two of her riding friends, who leaned in by each other and giggled about something. They didn't even notice Allison was in the ring.

Diamond Jack went around the course in perfect hunter style. He jumped smoothly and in stride. Allison rode him well. She patted Diamond Jack's neck when she came out of the ring. She had a huge smile on her face.

"Good job, Allison," Claire said. "Take him back to the barn. Leave his bridle on. You'll probably place."

"You were great." I walked alongside Allison while she rode Diamond Jack back to the barn. I patted his sweaty neck. "I hope old George goes as good as you did."

"Thanks. You'll do fine." Allison let Diamond Jack have loose reins as we walked along. "Hey, I forgot to tell you about the new kid who's going to be in our class this fall. Ingrid said she met him when she and David went to the movies the other night."

"He's probably a dork." I rolled my eyes.

"Ingrid said he's nice," Allison shifted her weight in the saddle. "Kinda cute."

I looked down.

What did Ingrid know about boys anyway?

"His family moved into my subdivision next door to David's house," Allison said. "His name is Tommy O'Connley? O'Connor? I don't know, something like that."

"You don't remember his name?" I asked.

"I know his first name is Tommy." Allison pulled back on the reins to stop Diamond Jack by the barn door when we reached our stabling area.

"Cassie, get George ready," Claire said when she caught up to Allison and me. "Where's Lisa? She goes right before you do."

Allison reached into her riding jacket pocket and pulled out a piece of gum. She tried to peel the wrapper off, but the pink gooey strings stuck to the paper. She pulled off as much of the pink goo as she could, popped it into her mouth, and shoved the crumpled wrapper back into her pocket. Then, she dismounted.

Warm, sticky gum? Super-gross.

21
MY TURN TO SHOW

GALLANT STAR STUCK HIS HEAD OUT of the stall door when the three of us and Diamond Jack walked inside the barn. He reached over the stall door to jingle the metal latch with his soft horse lips. I went over to him to stroke his forehead.

"Lisa's sitting in the bleachers in the front, or was, when Allison rode," I told Claire. I gave Gallant Star a final pat. I walked over to open George's stall door, put on a lead, and brought him out to put him on cross-ties.

"Allison, go and find Lisa." Claire opened Lisa's horse's stall door. "And tell Ingrid to join us. The class is almost over with. She needs to get Bailey to the ring in case she places."

Claire worked on Lisa's horse while I finished getting George ready. I brushed his coat. He looked shiny. Braids were in place yet. Keith came over by us when I was ready to put on George's saddle.

"Can I help?" he asked.

"You bet," Claire said. "Please finish grooming and tacking up Lisa's horse. I need to get Cassie on and warmed-up. You can help us at the ring."

"No problem." Keith took a finishing brush to Lisa's horse's coat.

I had George tacked up by the time Allison, Ingrid, and Lisa returned. I sat on the show trunk and pulled on my boots. They didn't go on very well. My feet were hot. Thank goodness they weren't super-new anymore, or I'd never get them on.

"Lisa, let's go," Claire said. "You needed to be here about fifteen minutes ago. Get your boots on. Keith will give you a leg up when you're ready. Come on, Cassie." She picked up Lisa's and my coat, and put them under her left arm. She put our gloves and show numbers in her right hand and headed out the door.

"I was paying attention to the time," Lisa said.

"No, you weren't." I tried to shove the short, frizzled hairs around my face into my riding helmet. "I saw you with your friends."

She made a squirmed-up face at me.

I gave her one back.

"Cassie!" Claire called from outside.

I led George outside. Claire gave me a leg up. I adjusted myself in the saddle and picked up my reins. I barely had to press George's sides. He walked so fast toward the warm-up ring.

Why doesn't he ever move like this at home?

"Oh, Cassie, dear!" A familiar voice shouted out my name. I turned to my left and saw Grandma Leona, Mom, and Dad making their way through the horses and riders. Grandma Leona waved at me. I had to pull twice on the reins to get George to stop. He bobbed his head up and down and pulled against the bit, trying to get some extra rein length, but I held him firmly.

"Hey, Cass," Mom and Dad said together.

"Hi, you're just in time," I said. "I'm warming-up before it's my turn."

"Oh, good, I didn't want to miss seeing your first trip." Grandma Leona said. She fanned herself with a floppy show schedule and squeezed my lower leg with the other hand.

I was glad Grandma Leona was there. She always made me feel better. She had on a wide-collared, lemon-yellow, knee-length dress and white low-heeled shoes with golden buckles. Her wide-brimmed straw hat, with a white ribbon and bow tied around it, had a small cluster of red fake flowers on its right side. She carried her big white purse—the one with the rose-shaped golden clasp on it. I smelled her powdery perfume. She always wore lots of it.

"What's on your new shirt?" Mom scowled. She wore her paisley short-sleeve shirt and tan bell-bottom pants along with her favorite pair of old brown leather loafers she always wore around the horses. Her long, dark hair was pulled back into a smooth ponytail.

I brushed my left hand across the stain on my shirt front. "I got all sweaty and full of hay chaff. I tried to get it off."

"It's just a little dirt, Joanne," Grandma Leona said. "I'm sure it will come out in the wash."

It was weird when Grandma Leona called Mom by her first name.

"How are things going?" Dad asked. He wore a light blue T-shirt, dark gray pants, and black leather loafers. He patted George's neck.

"Okay," I said.

"Busy," Claire said. "I'm glad you could come to watch. Now, I'd love to stay and talk, but I need Cassie to warm-up George. You can stay here and watch if you like, or you can find a seat on the bleachers. We're riding in the front ring."

"Mother, let's find some shade for you," Mom said to Grandma Leona. "We'll find a seat on the bleachers."

"I could use a lemonade," Grandma Leona said. "Let's stop at the food truck and get something cool to drink. Cassie, dear, good luck. We're rooting for you." She smiled and squeezed my leg again.

"Ed, are you coming with us?" Mom asked.

"I'll stay here and watch," Dad said. "I'll meet up with you after the class. Claire, can I help?"

George shifted his weight and pulled against the bit again. "I have to get ready Dad. George is getting antsy "

"Here, take her coat and gloves." Claire handed them to Dad. "Okay, Cassie, go and warm-up."

George practically bolted to the practice ring. I had to pay attention and get him under control. The other horses and riders were busy doing their own warming-up. They wouldn't watch out for me.

After trotting around the ring a few times, George settled down. He cantered smoothly when I pressed my leg on him. He even picked up the correct lead. Everything was fine until a chestnut horse and rider cut me off when I turned out of the far corner. I had to pull George up fast. He got all rattled.

"Lisa! Watch where you're going!" Claire shouted.

"Sorry." Lisa gave me a fake smile when she rode past me again. She trotted to the other side of the ring.

I shot her a look.

"Settle George down before you come over the practice fence," Claire said.

I had to stroke George's neck a few more times before he calmed down. Anytime another horse crossed in front of him, he'd throw his head up and not pay attention to me for a while.

"Okay, try the fence," Claire said.

I cantered George around the turn and came at the fence. He chipped-in right in front of the fence, but at least he jumped it.

"Come again, and this time use more leg on him. Keep him moving forward," Claire said.

"I'm trying to." Sweat tickled the sides of my face. My shirt was completely pasted to my back. I set George up a second time, and he jumped it fine.

"Good girl, Cass," Dad said.

I forgot Dad was there. I was so busy trying to ride George.

"One more time and then to the front ring," Claire said. "Lisa, get ready to jump the fence next."

I rode George around again, and he jumped smoothly. I pulled him up and walked him over by Dad, Keith, and Claire. George stood like a statue while Keith wiped his sweat off with the towel.

"Can I use the towel?" I took off my helmet.

"Sure, if you don't mind some horse sweat," Keith said as he handed me the dirty towel.

I wiped off my face, my arms, and the back of my neck. I handed the towel back to Keith. He wiped off my boots with it. I put my helmet back on, not caring if my hair frizzles stood out, and managed to get my riding jacket on after Dad handed it to me. I tied my show number around my waist. I'd wait and try to put my gloves on down by the ring. I wasn't even sure if I could get them on.

"Ed, there's a horse I want you to see," Stan said as he walked up to us. "Talked to a trainer friend of mine who said he's got a nice chestnut gelding for sale in your price range. Good hunter for Cassie. Can be a bit hot to begin with, nothing dangerous though, just needs some lunging before he's worked. He's off the track but has had a lot of schooling since they first brought him home."

"Is he okay?" Dad asked. "He's not dangerous, is he?"

"He's warming up right now," Stan said. "He's approaching the practice fence closest to us."

We watched as a chestnut horse with a white star, wide blaze down his nose, and white hind socks jumped a practice fence. He cantered around and took the second fence as nicely as he did the first fence.

"Hey, that's the same horse I saw this morning when we drove into the stable!" I said. George reached around to brush off a fly on his shoulder. "Keith said hi to the horse's groom, who had finished lunging him when we got here."

"Jumped good," Stan said. "Nice rounded form. He's in the Adult Amateur Class. Can talk to the trainer if you want to look at him."

"What do you think, Cassie?" Dad asked me. "I'm not crazy that he's a bit hot, but he looks good."

"Wouldn't even consider him if I thought he'd be too much horse for Cassie to handle," Stan said. "Seen the horse before at shows. Didn't know he was for sale until today."

"Can we look at him?" I asked. Claire waved at me and pointed toward the front ring. "Dad, I have to go to the ring now."

"If you think he'll be decent for Cassie, we'll consider him," Dad said. "Your mom can see him too."

"And Grandma Leona," I said.

"I'll tell the trainer we'll look at the horse," Stan turned toward the practice ring, "Good luck, Cassie."

"Thanks." I picked up the reins and nudged George.

I couldn't wait to tell Allison and Ingrid that I get to look at another new horse.

"By the way, I saw what Lisa did." Dad walked next to George and me. "Lousy thing to do."

"She always does that." I found a spot among the remaining riders and horses who still waited to go. I pulled up George. "She knows George gets rattled when he gets cut off."

"He seems all right now." Dad ran his hand down George's shoulder. George turned his head to look at Dad.

"You know, you can watch Gallant Star in his jumper class today," I said. "He goes after lunch. I still have my second class over fences this afternoon and my flat class after that, but I hope I can see him go. We can watch him show together."

"Do you need something to drink?" Dad asked, totally ignoring what I had just said to him.

"Maybe some lemonade." My shoulders slumped. I looked down and picked at the woven leather lace on my rein.

"Be right back." Dad walked over to the food truck.

As I watched the other riders, I practically melted in my jacket as I waited for my turn. I tried to put on my gloves, which looked like crumpled black spiders. I even straightened out the fingers to get my hand in them, but they didn't stay straightened out. I wiped my hands on my jacket front a few times, but that didn't work either. After I wrestled them on, I had to make fists a few times to stretch them out. That didn't help much.

"Here." Dad handed me a plastic cup of lemonade. I could barely hold onto it because my gloves were tight.

I gulped it down and handed him the cup. "Thanks."

Lisa pulled up her horse next to me. Keith and Claire stood by Dad, George, and me.

"Where are we in the order?" Claire asked.

"I don't know," I said. "I think it's my turn in maybe two or three riders?"

Claire went over to the fence to check the show order. She looked at the rider in the ring and came back over.

"Lisa, you're on deck. Cassie, you're after her." Claire took the towel from Keith and wiped off Lisa's boots and her horse.

The horse and rider in the ring finished up and came out through the gate. Lisa was next.

"Wish me luck!" Lisa nudged her horse and pulled on his rein.

Like she needed any.

"Good luck," Keith said.

"Do your best," Claire said.

Dad crossed his arms.

I turned to look out toward the bleachers. Mom and Grandma Leona talked to each other. Grandma Leona looked up, smiled at me, and held up both of her hands. Her fingers were crossed. I smiled and waved back.

Ingrid and Allison walked up to me, leading their horses. They both had their jackets, helmets, and gloves on with their show numbers tied around their waists.

"Did you go yet?" Ingrid asked.

"No, I go when Lisa's done," I said.

"Good luck," Allison said. She popped a pink bubble.

"Yes, good luck," Ingrid said.

Lisa rode out of the ring. She had a big smile on her face and patted her horse on his neck. Her trip wasn't that good, but she must have thought it was.

"Lisa, pull your saddle," Claire said. "Stand by for the placing. Cassie, just keep George moving forward, and you'll do great."

"Have fun, Cass." Dad smiled up at me.

I let out a deep breath. I pulled on the right rein, nudged George into a trot, and headed toward the in-gate. As I entered the ring, I made a circle and then stopped to face the judge. I was given the go ahead and cued George to pick up his left canter lead. George arched his neck and actually behaved like a show horse. I rode along the fence and slightly to the left when I reached the end of the ring. I turned George toward the first fence. He jumped it at the right take-off spot!

Good, only seven more fences to go.

I cut through turned to my left and sent George down to the next two fences. They were on a diagonal line across the center of the ring. He took each one in stride. I squeezed my right fingers on the rein and George turned for the next two fences that were set up along the side of the ring. Again, he did a good job.

Keep it up, Georgie Boy.

I rode across the center of the ring, and we jumped the diagonal sixth fence. I squeezed my left fingers and turned George toward the last two fences. They were along the side of the ring in front of the bleachers. George came around the corner and headed for the final fences.

Come on, George. You can do it. We're almost done.

Over fence seven and only a few more strides to ... fence eight. *Done. Whew!* He did it without chipping-in, stopping, or dumping me in the ring in front of everyone!

"That's my girl!" Grandma Leona shouted.

Dad whistled when I rode past him. I smiled and patted George on the neck as I cantered a circle. Even

George must have known he did a good job. He arched his neck and cantered smoothly. I pulled him up to a walk and left through the in-gate. The final rider rode in past me.

"Great job, Cassie," Claire said as she unbuckled the girth and slid the saddle off after I had dismounted. "That's the best I've ever seen you and George go. Keith, can I have the towel?" She traded Keith the towel for my saddle and went to work wiping off George.

"Did you see how good George went?" I said. "I can't believe he's the same horse I take lessons on!"

"You were great," Allison said. Diamond Jack rubbed his left ear on her right shoulder. He shook his head when he was done scratching against her.

"You probably won," Ingrid said. Bailey whinnied to another horse across the driveway.

Lisa looked out toward the ring. Her horse swished flies with his tail.

"Oh, I don't know." I ran my hand down old Georgie's nose.

"Good job, Cass," Dad said. He came over by me and put his hand on my right shoulder. He squeezed gently.

"Thanks, Dad," I said.

"Cassie, walk George to cool him down a bit," Claire said as she handed the reins to me. "But stay close by. Everybody else ready?"

George and I walked up and down the driveway a few times until the judge had the results. I wiped my face off with my gloved hand. Sweat dripped down my back. I couldn't wait to peel off my coat. Claire waved me over.

We all stood together.

"First place, number 708 ..."

I never heard the rest of it.

I won! Ha! I beat Lisa!

I led George to the in-gate and pulled on the reins, "Come on, George." I clucked to him to get him to trot in. I trotted him across the ring to where the judge and his attendant stood.

"Nice job, young lady," the judge said to me. The attendant smiled at me and handed the judge the blue rosette ribbon from the six different colored ribbons she held in her left hand. The judge hung the blue ribbon on George's bridle by the brow band. George snorted a bit and arched his neck.

"Thank you," I said.

As I walked George out of the ring, I looked behind me. Allison had placed second. Lisa was third. Ingrid was fifth. I didn't know who the fourth and sixth place riders were. At least we all won ribbons.

I waited for Allison and Ingrid before I walked back to the barn. I let George take a mouthful of grass from the lawn by the ring while I took off my helmet. I held it between my knees as I peeled off my gloves and shoved them into my coat pockets. I knew

I had helmet-head hair, but I didn't care. I wiped off my forehead with the back of my jacket sleeve. I took off my coat next. The sleeves got turned inside out because the shiny polyester lining stuck to my sweaty arms.

"Do you want me to take something, Cass?" Dad asked.

"You can carry all of this." I handed him my riding stuff. George rubbed his head against me. He got some more green horse schlob on my shirt and the top of my breeches. It sort of matched the first stain on my shirt. I wiped at it with my hand, but it only made the stain worse.

"You won!" Grandma Leona said. She and Mom had walked up to us. She hugged me even though I was pretty sweaty. I smelled like her perfume after she let me go. "You did such a good job."

"Great job, Cass." Mom hugged me too. She looked down at the two new stains when she let me go, but didn't say anything.

"Let's get these horses back to the barn and out of the sun," Claire said. "Ingrid, come on."

Ingrid had been talking to her parents and Allison's and some other people I couldn't see. Bailey stood in the way. Her family and mine talked to each other as they followed along beside her and Bailey. Lisa had given her horse to Keith and headed off with her two older riding friends.

Like it was some big surprise that she wouldn't care for her own horse before or after a class.

Allison and I led the group back to the barn.

"I'm glad you beat Lisa," I said.

"I'm glad YOU beat Lisa," Allison said. "Did you see her face? All pouty." She tipped her head and made a face like Lisa had, only her lower lip poked out more.

"She thinks she can get on and ride a perfect round, but she hardly puts any time into practicing anymore. Just because she has a push-button show horse doesn't mean she'll win every class she enters," I said.

"She thinks she's so great," Allison said. She blew a pink bubble.

"I know, but she's not," I said. "Hey, remember that chestnut horse we saw when we pulled into the show?"

"Chestnut horse?" Allison asked.

"You know, the one that was all sweaty and hot from being lunged." I said. "Keith said hi to the groom. Remember?"

"Oh, the one with the big white blaze down its nose." Allison moved her hand up and down so it looked like she had a blaze that ran down her nose.

"Yes, that one," I said. "Turns out, he's for sale. Stan talked to Dad by the warm-up ring when I was getting ready for my class. We're going to look at him.

He's sort of hot, but Stan said he wouldn't be too much horse for me."

"He's hot?" Allison swooshed a fly away from Diamond Jack's face.

"Well, I guess he needs to be lunged or turned out first before anyone can get on him. He's off the track." I wiped off my forehead with my hand. Fuzzy little hairs stuck up all around the sides of my face. I tried to flatten them with my palm, but I knew it didn't help.

"Hey, maybe he'll finally be your horse," Allison said.

"Maybe." I smiled and walked George into the barn.

22
RUNNING INTO TROUBLE

I REMOVED GEORGE'S BLUE RIBBON to hang up on the stable's banner. One blue, two red, one yellow, one white, and two pink ribbons were already hanging along the top of the stable banner from the Adult Amateur Owner riders' first two classes. I lay the blue ribbon on the show trunk and put George away in his stall. I had to stand on the show trunk to hang up my ribbon. I pushed a few of them apart to make room for mine. I was about to get down when everyone who had been behind Allison and me walked into the barn and filled up the aisle.

"Hi, Cassie." David walked next to Ingrid as she passed by, leading Bailey.

"Hi, David."

David's here? Great, now what?

I jumped off of the show trunk. I pretended to be busy putting away my stuff after Dad handed it to me. I folded my riding coat around my left arm and held it in front of my shirt stains when Ingrid, David, and Allison stood by me. I ran my right hand over the top of my hair.

Why wouldn't my hair stop sticking up and frizzing?

"So, how'd you do?" David asked me. He wore a dark blue T-shirt, cut-off jean shorts, black tennis shoes, and tube socks that he had hiked up to his knees.

"I—"

"She won the class." Ingrid cut me off. Her face was all pink and smiley. Her hair was flattened to her head worse than mine from wearing her helmet.

I can answer David's questions myself, thank you very much, Ingrid.

"She beat Lisa," Allison said after she popped a bubble. She pointed back and forth to me and her with her index finger. "We beat Lisa."

"You should have seen Lisa, all sour-puss and everything," Ingrid said. She moved closer to David.

"She doesn't like losing." David turned his head and smiled at her. "Hey, I'm starved. Do you guys have time to get something to eat?

"Sure," Allison said.

"I need a soda," Ingrid said.

"I might—"

"Cassie, Stan wants us to watch Napoleon go." Dad interrupted me as he walked up to us. "He's in a class in the indoor."

"Who's Napoleon?" Ingrid asked.

"A horse that's for sale," I said. "We're going to look at him."

"We saw him when we first got to the show," Allison said. She popped a small bubble.

"You're getting a horse?" David asked me.

"I—"

"Hopefully she is," Ingrid cut me off again. "It's taking long enough for her to get one. Come on, let's go. See you later alligator." She took David's hand. They walked out of the barn.

"I'll get Stan. He's down by the boarders." Dad frowned toward Ingrid and then walked away to get him.

Mom and Grandma Leona stood in front of Gallant Star's stall door. Gallant nuzzled each of them for a treat.

"Cassie, who's this?" Mom ran her hand down his nose and then brushed his forelock aside. She ran her finger around the edge of his star. "Look at this, a perfectly shaped star."

"He or she has a lovely temperament," Grandma Leona said as Gallant Star turned his nose toward her. He nuzzled her outstretched hand. He reached for her purse, but she moved it away from him. "Oh, no you don't, you rascal."

"That's Gallant Star, you know, the horse that Dad won't buy for me." I held out my hand to Gallant Star. He wiggled his soft horse lips across my right palm. "Wait, what do you mean a perfect diamond? His star is lopsided."

"No, it's a perfect diamond shape. See?" Mom pushed the forelock aside for me. "I thought your dad said he was too thin, scraggly-like. He looks fine to me." She looked into the stall and checked out Gallant Star.

"Oh, so this is the mystery horse you've been telling me about," Grandma Leona said. Gallant Star lifted his head, perked up his ears, and whinnied to a horse outside the barn door. "You were right, Cassie, he sure is a beauty. You know, Joanne, he sort of reminds me of your favorite school horse. The one you used to ride when you were about Cassie's age. What was her name? Lady something?"

"Miss Lady Jane." Mom smiled. Gallant Star rubbed his nose against her shoulder.

"Gallant Star's a lot better than when we first saw him," I said. "I told you he's healthier now. He's jumping in the class this afternoon. We can watch him go, unless I have to ride in my next class the same time he goes."

Why did his star look different? Maybe I didn't remember what it really looked like.

"I'd like to see him ridden," Grandma Leona said.

"I would as well." Mom turned to Dad, who had walked up to us. "Ed, can you tell me again why we aren't considering Gallant Star for Cassie? He seems like a nice horse." She let Gallant Star nuzzle her hand.

"Well, he didn't look so hot when we first saw him, and I haven't seen him jump yet." Dad stood with his arms crossed.

"You can watch him after lunch when he competes in his jumping class," I said.

"Well, right now, Stan needs us to watch Napoleon." Dad turned and headed down the aisle. "We're supposed to meet up with him and someone named Luke at the indoor ring. I guess that's the horse's owner or trainer. Come on."

Mom, Grandma Leona, and I followed along behind Dad to the indoor riding ring. We had to watch out for all of the Adult Amateur Owner riders and their horses as they rode to and from the show ring. When we walked inside and despite the open doors and roof shade, it was even hotter in the indoor ring. We joined Dad, Stan, and a man with a steel-gray crew-cut who wore blue jeans, cowboy boots, and a green T-shirt that had Wild River Acres written across the front in white letters. Grandma Leona stood near him and fanned herself with her droopy show schedule. Mom wiped off her forehead with the back of her hand. I used both palms to flatten down my hair. I pulled at the front of my riding shirt to try and fan myself. It didn't help.

"This is Luke, Napoleon's trainer," Stan said. Everyone shook hands with him. "He can answer any questions you might have."

"Is this the young lady you're buying him for?" Luke asked as he leaned in toward me and shook my right hand.

Oh, super-duper-gross! His breath smelled like mothballs. His hand was all spongy and sweaty.

I fake-smiled. When he let go of my hand, I pressed my palm against my leg so I wouldn't be rude and wipe it off in front of him. I stepped back over by Mom.

"So, what's the story about him?" Dad asked. "Why are you selling him?"

"He's been an Adult Amateur Owner's horse for a few years." Luke crossed his arms. "His owner wants to move to Florida and live near her son, daughter-in-law, and new baby. You know, first grandchild and all. She doesn't want to take the horse with her. Her family lives in Tampa? Miami? I don't know, somewhere. She just wants to dote on that new baby, I guess. She'll be riding him in this class. She's up pretty soon ... they're by the ring now ... he's the chestnut with the broad blaze and white hind socks."

Mrs. Wagner had finished her turn in the ring on her pudgy gray mare and walked out. Keith took her reins and talked to Jody, Napoleon's groom, who stood right next to them. Jody wiped off of Napoleon and then his rider's boots. The rider nudged Napoleon into a trot and into the ring. She asked him to canter and started to ride the hunter course.

"See, he's consistent and smooth," Luke said. "Nice round top line over the fences."

"Hmm ... he looks good," Dad said.

"Like his stride," Stan said. "Covers ground smoothly."

"Seems like a good possibility for Cass," Mom said.

Grandma Leona watched Napoleon's trip. She squinted and pressed her lips together.

"Do I get to ride him today?" I asked.

"How about you take him home for a few days to try him out?" Luke said. "His owner won't mind. She's going out of town for a while anyway. I have to be honest with you, I've got someone north of Chicago who's possibly interested in him, but she's not budging on her offer. First person with the money gets the horse in my book, if you know what I mean."

"Got room in a trailer today. He can come with us." Stan watched as Napoleon walked out of the ring. He turned to Dad. "That is, if you want to consider him. He's in your price range."

"Sure, let's try him out." Dad nodded. "Cassie can spend some time with him, see how he behaves on the ground as well as when she's riding him." He smiled at me.

I smiled back.

"No problems with his behavior." Luke squeezed Stan's shoulder. "He's a perfect gentleman."

Grandma Leona adjusted her purse on her right arm and said, "But what about Gallant—"

"Cassie, you need to get ready for your next class," Claire said. She seemed out of breath when she caught up to us. "Please find Allison and Ingrid, and tell them to come to the barn pronto. Let Lisa know, too, if you see her. Stan, Mrs. O'Mally needs your help with the boarders."

"I think Allison and Ingrid might still be by the food truck," I said. "Can I have some money for a lemonade?"

"Here, Cass." Mom pulled out a five-dollar bill from her purse and gave it to me. "Make sure you eat something. You didn't have any breakfast."

"Mom—"

"Go!" Mom said.

I cut through the indoor ring along the far wall and made my way through the crowd to the outside door. I headed straight for the food truck, but didn't see Allison, Ingrid, or David. I bought a hot dog with only ketchup on it and two lemonades in white paper cups. I took three bites of the hot dog and carried it in my left hand while I balanced the two lemonades in my right hand. I walked to the front ring to see if Allison and Ingrid were sitting up in the bleachers, but I still didn't see them. I headed back toward our barn.

As I dodged the horses and riders and I tried to take a sip from one of my lemonade cups, I was suddenly bumped hard on my left side. "Ow ... hey!" My hot dog was knocked to the ground, and the lemonades splashed all over my hand.

"Watch where you're going, kid!" shouted a man about Keith's age. He had dark shoulder-length hair and pork chop sideburns, like Elvis Presley's. He wore a tie-dyed T-shirt, bell-bottom jeans, and old work boots. He pushed up his aviator sunglasses, took a long drag off of his cigarette, and blew the smoke in my face. "Beat it, kid!"

"You ran into—" I backed away from his smoke. I backed away from him. The hair on my arms and under my braid felt tight and creepy. My stomach tightened.

"Yeah, beat it, kid," said the other guy with him, who was about the same age as the first one. He had greasy blond hair pulled back into a ponytail, and a beard and mustache that looked like the hippies I'd seen on TV or in magazines. He wore a brown T-shirt, bell-bottom blue jeans, and scuffed up cowboy boots. His yellowed, crooked teeth showed when he grinned.

"I'm not a—"

A tri-colored Corgi dog, trotting past us with its owner, pulled against its leash, snatched up my hot dog, and gobbled it up.

"Get," Elvis Chops leaned in, "lost." He took a drag from the cigarette and again blew the smoke at me. He flicked his lit cigarette toward the main barn's wall.

"Yeah, get lost," Hippie Hair said. He giggled like a girl.

"Stupid kid," Elvis Chops said.

"Yeah, stupid kid," Hippie Hair said.

They walked away toward the food truck.

"You could start a fire, dumbheads!" I pounced on the burning cigarette and ground it with my toe. Once I was sure it was out, I raced toward the back barn. I still held onto what was left of my two cups of lemonade. It splashed out as I wove in and out and between the horses and riders. My heart was beating like crazy. I slowed down a bit when I got inside the open barn door. Mom and Grandma Leona stood in front of Gallant Star's stall door while Mom stroked his nose.

"Cassie, why on earth are you running in this heat?" Grandma Leona reached out to me, touching my arm.

"Are you all right?" Mom asked.

"I have ... to ... get ready." My hand shook slightly as I drank the rest of the lemonade in one of the cups and started drinking from the other one. When I finished, I crushed both cups and threw them in the trash barrel. My hands still shook when I opened the latch on George's stall door.

23
GALLANT STAR'S TURN TO SHOW

MY SECOND CHILDREN'S HUNT SEAT Equitation Over
Fences class didn't go as well as my first one. Old
George must have been tired from the show excite-
ment and performed only a little better than he did at
home. I was the first to ride in the class. I forgot to
count the strides in between the fences, so George
ended up chipping-in at two fences—the brush box
and the oxer. I lost my balance and right stirrup both
times. Claire told me to put him away until it was
time for my last class—Children's Hunt Seat Equitation on the Flat, which followed the over-fences class
we had been riding in.

I wouldn't be in the ribbons this time. I didn't
care. Now I could watch Gallant Star in his jumping
class, or at least until I had to get ready to ride in the
flat class. I walked George back to the barn while
Allison, Ingrid, and Lisa waited their turn to show in
the front ring. Keith and Stan had Gallant Star on
cross-ties when I led George inside the barn aisle.

"How'd it go?" Keith brushed Gallant Star's coat
until it was a brilliant red. He stopped to clean out
the brush he was using with a black rubber curry
comb.

"He chipped-in at two fences." I removed George's tack once I had him back in his stall.

"Awe, that's too bad. Better luck next time." Keith gave Gallant Star a going-over with a towel. Gallant Star stood like a statue. His ears were perked up. He occasionally snorted. Maybe he knew it was his turn to show.

"George will be George," Stan said. "Can't change them, even for a show day. I'll get Gallant Star's tack." Stan came back with his saddle, bridle, white bell boots to protect his front hooves, and dark brown leather boots with felt linings to protect his front legs in case he knocked down a rail while jumping in the class.

Once Gallant Star was tacked up, Keith led him outside. Stan followed behind with Joe McLaine, who would ride Gallant in his jumping class. Keith gave Joe a leg up, and the three of them headed toward the warm-up ring.

"Will you grab Joe's show coat and number and meet us by the ring?" Stan said to Keith.

"Be right there." Keith went back to the barn to get the gear.

There were plenty of horses and riders getting ready for the jumper class. The jumper riders had taken over half of the warm-up ring because the fences were now set up higher than the 2-foot, 6-inch ones I had ridden over earlier. I watched Joe ride Gallant Star around the practice ring. Gallant Star's neck was arched, and he looked like he meant business. His coat flashed red in the sunlight. His black mane and tail flowed like silk. He certainly looked like a star.

"There you are," Grandma Leona said as she, Mom, and Dad walked up to me, each one carrying two cups of lemonade. She handed me one of hers. "We're not too late to see your mystery horse go, are we?"

"No, they're warming him up in the ring. See? He's on the far end." I pointed to where Gallant Star and Joe were. "The jumper class starts in a few minutes. Gallant Star goes fourth."

"Oh, good, I didn't want to miss this," Grandma Leona said. She fanned herself with her tattered, floppy show schedule. "He IS stunning."

"He moves and listens to Joe's instructions nicely," Mom said.

"He's great to ride," I said. I finished drinking the first cup of lemonade. Mom then handed me one of hers. I slurped it down and stacked the two paper cups together.

"I have to admit he looks a lot better than when we first saw him, Cass, and when I saw him at the barn." Dad watched them.

"Look at them take the fence," Grandma Leona said. "He certainly is talented."

Stan schooled Joe and Gallant Star over a few of the practice fences. Gallant soared over them beautifully.

"Yes, he is," Mom said.

Dad drank his lemonade.

"That's enough," Stan said. "Let's clean him up."

Stan, Keith, Gallant Star, and Joe walked over by us. Keith handed Joe his coat and number and wiped the sweat off of Gallant's face and neck with a towel. Gallant Star rubbed his head against my shoulder. I straightened his forelock when he was done scratching.

"We're ready for the first jumper!" called out the official man at the ring's gate. "Next rider on deck!"

"Be good," I said to Gallant Star. He bobbed his head as if he knew what I said. I patted him on his neck. "Good luck, Joe."

"Have a safe ride." Grandma Leona gave Gallant Star a pat on the shoulder.

"Have fun." Mom ran her hand down Gallant Star's nose.

Dad crossed his arms.

"Thanks, everyone." Joe turned Gallant Star toward the in-gate to watch the first few horses and riders jump the course. Stan had said there were 17 horses entered. Stan and Keith stood next to them. Grandma Leona, Mom, Dad, and I squeezed in at the fence to watch.

The first two horses and riders jumped a clean round, well within the allowed time limit. The second horse and rider pulled down two rails on the triple combination. The spectators who sat in the bleachers and stood along the fence all said "Oh!" at the same time.

When the horse and rider left the ring, Joe trotted Gallant Star into the ring. Gallant Star arched his neck and stretched out his stride. He snorted a bit. Joe brought him to a halt and waited to be given the signal to start. Joe bowed his head to the judge's area. He was told to begin. Joe asked Gallant Star to canter, and the electronic clock started the minute they crossed the starting line.

I held my breath and gripped the fence board as I watched Joe head Gallant Star toward the first fence.

Gallant Star easily jumped the first big oxer and headed toward the tall single rail. He snorted with each hand-gallop stride as he made his way over the second fence and onto the wide Swedish oxer at fence three. He then galloped down to fence four—the narrow oxer—and went on to jump the triple bar with plenty of room to spare. Fence six—the in and out—wasn't a problem at all. Joe turned Gallant Star toward the seventh fence—another big oxer—and jumped it cleanly. Next was the liverpool. It was supposed to look like a pool of water on the ground, but the water was really a piece of blue plastic between two rail jumps. Gallant Star shot over it like a rocket and headed toward the triple combination— the fence the last horse and rider had had four faults on.

I barely breathed as they approached the three 4-foot high fences in a row.

First fence—clean.

Second fence—clean.

Third fence—clean.

Only one more fence to go. I gripped the fence board even tighter.

Joe headed Gallant Star toward the last tall vertical fence and—clean!

Joe patted Gallant's neck as he let him gallop past the in-gate, turned him toward the center of the ring, gently pulled him up to a posting trot, and then to a walk. Everyone around us applauded. Keith whistled.

"He did it!" I shouted. I let go of the fence board and then jumped up and down in place a few times.

"He sure did," Grandma Leona said. She smiled at me.

"Now he'll be in the jump-off for sure, if there's one," I said. "Dad, wasn't he great?"

Dad crumpled his white paper cup with his left hand. "Yes, Cass, he had a nice round, but there will probably be a jump-off. The fences will get higher and the times faster and the turns sharper. Can he handle that? Could you?"

Sweat trickled down the back of my neck as I stared back at him. "I ..."

I didn't know how long it would take me to be able to ride Gallant Star like he needed to be ridden if he was my horse. I wanted to learn. I'd work hard. Didn't that count for something? Why was Dad being so mean to me?

Mom frowned at him. "Oh, Ed, stop being so—"

Dad held up his right hand. "I'm just saying—"

"Ed, be a sport," Grandma Leona said. "This is Cassie's day. Let her have some fun."

We walked over to where Stan, Keith, Gallant Star and Joe were standing. Joe had dismounted and taken off his jacket and helmet. Keith loosened the girth and got ready to walk Gallant Star to cool him down a bit, or at least to get his breathing back to normal again. Gallant Star puffed through his nostrils.

"Take Gallant Star to the barn and run a sponge of cool water on his face, along his lower neck, and between his hindquarters," Stan said. "Should help bring down his body heat. Walk him in the barn and out of the sun until we're ready to go in the jump-off. Joe and I will watch the class."

"Will do." Keith led Gallant Star toward the back barn.

"I'd like to see some more of this class," Grandma Leona said. She looked at Dad and Mom.

"So would I." Mom turned back toward the ring when the sound of a pole fell off when the horse competing pulled it down. The crowd gasped.

"Cassie, Claire asked me to find you," Ingrid rode up on Bailey. Her cheeks were deep pink. She must have given her coat to Claire because she didn't have it on. David walked beside her. "Our class is almost over with. You need to bring George to the ring for the last flat class."

"Hey, you should have seen Gallant Star go!" I jumped up a bit. "He was great! He'll be in the jump-off if there's one."

"What's a jump-off?" David asked.

"It's when—" I started to say, but Ingrid cut me off. I flattened my hair down with my hands and then crossed my arms.

"When the horses and riders in a jumping class have all gone in the first round," Ingrid said. Bailey stamped his front right hoof to get a fly off his leg, "only the horses without any faults, either by taking down poles or taking too much time to finish the course, come back to compete again by having to jump fewer jumps and having to go faster than the first time they were in the ring. Whoever goes the fastest and has the fewest poles down wins." Bailey pulled the reins down from Ingrid's grip and rubbed his nose on his right front leg where the fly had bitten him. She collected the reins when he was finished.

"Oh." David swatted away a horse fly from his head. He looked miserable.

"I'll meet you at the ring," I said to Ingrid.

"Are you almost done riding today?" David asked Ingrid. "I think I'm getting sunburned."

Ingrid turned Bailey around and headed to the front ring. David followed by Bailey's side.

"Yes, this is my last class ..."

I couldn't hear them anymore as they walked away.

"Let's walk down and watch Cassie in her last class when she's ready to go," Grandma Leona said. "We can catch some of the horses and riders going now before the jump-off."

"You can stay here if you want." I turned toward the barn. "I'm just riding in a flat class."

"Come and get us when you're ready to go to the front ring," Dad said.

Rats! I wanted to watch Gallant Star in the jump-off, but now that I had to ride George, I probably wouldn't get to see him. Maybe if my flat class went fast enough I would still have time to watch him go again.

Keith had Gallant Star on cross-ties in the barn aisle. The big bay wasn't puffing anymore. Keith had wiped off Gallant Star's sweat with a wet towel. Keith put the saddle back on Gallant Star and gently tightened the girth.

"Are you riding now?" Keith asked me.

"Yes. I have to get George ready. At least it's the last class of the day. I wanted to see Gallant Star in the jump-off though." I opened George's stall door.

Super-great. George had been scratching his braids again!

"George!" All that was left of the five braids closest to his bridle path was a mass of wavy mane fuzz. He only turned his head toward me and chewed some hay.

"Did he rub out his braids again?" Keith asked me.

"He always does this!" I led him out of his stall and put him on the pair of cross-ties down from the ones Gallant Star was on. I started to brush him off.

"Well, at least it's the end of the day." Keith undid Gallant Star's cross-ties and led him toward the open barn door. "Just clean him up the best you can. You're almost done."

"I know there's nothing I can do now … hey, wait." I walked over to Gallant Star and gave him a hug around his neck. "Good luck, boy. You can beat them."

Keith walked Gallant Star out toward the back ring, and I finished getting George ready.

I never got to see Gallant Star go again. By the time I was ready to ride George down to the ring, they had announced the horses and riders who would compete in the jump-off. I was pretty sure I also saw Elvis Chops and Hippie Hair hanging out around the spectators by the back ring as I rode past and up toward the front ring. I shuttered when I saw them.

Once I was in the front ring along with the other eighteen horses and riders in the flat class, I tried to concentrate on my equitation. But George poked along even though I dug my heels into his sides. He barely cantered smoothly enough for me to sit comfortably on him. I didn't place. Allison won the class, Lisa was second, and Ingrid finished fourth. All of us—except Lisa—dismounted, loosened our girths, and walked our horses back to the barn to help cool them down. Lisa made some excuse about having to leave with her parents and handed her horse over to Claire.

"Must be time to pack up if Lisa disappeared." I took off my helmet and held it in my left hand as we walked along.

"She sure knows how to get out of doing any work." Allison wadded up another piece of warm bubble gum from her coat pocket and plopped it into her mouth. She chewed a bit and then blew a big pink bubble. It popped onto her chin. She picked it off and put the gum back into her mouth.

More hot gum? Still super-gross.

"Do you want to sleep over tonight?" I asked Allison. "I can see if Ingrid wants to come too."

"Sure, I'll ask my mom, but I think Ingrid has another date with David tonight. They're leaving right after we get back to the barn." Allison took off her helmet and wiped her forehead off with the back of her right, coat sleeve.

"She's not helping either?" My face suddenly felt flushed and hot.

"No. She said Keith can put Bailey away." Allison wiped a fly away from Diamond Jack's face.

"But he'll have Gallant Star to cool down," I said. "I'll help with Bailey. Keith has enough to do."

"I'll help too." Allison led Diamond Jack into the barn.

Stan, Joe, Keith, Mrs. O'Mally, Allison's parents, Ingrid's parents, and some other people I didn't know were all standing around Gallant Star, who was standing on the cross-ties. Everyone seemed pretty happy. Stan held onto a long blue ribbon.

Gallant Star must have won!

"Girls, you should have seen him go," Keith said to us as our horses' hooves clomped on the barn aisle floor. "He was terrific."

"Nice horse you've got here, Stan. Where'd you get him?" a man I didn't know asked.

"Bought him back in early June." Stan patted Gallant Star's shoulder. "Was in rough shape when we got him, but came along nicely. Thought we'd see what he could do at a show."

"Super-nice jumper," the man said. "Thinking of selling him?"

"Not now. Don't know what he can do yet. This is only a schooling show. Need to see what he can do against the big boys at an A-rated show. He's got the talent." Stan laid the ribbon on the top of the show tack trunk.

"Let me know when you want to sell him," the man said. He headed out of the barn.

Dad, Mom, and Grandma Leona had walked into the barn and joined the others crowded around Gallant Star.

"Did he win?" Grandma Leona asked.

"Yes, and he was a dream to ride," Joe said. "He did everything I asked him to do. Wow, what a cat when he made his turns in the jump-off."

"Okay, everybody, let's get these horses taken care of," Stan announced to us. "Been a long enough day for all of us. Start packing up your gear when you untack your horses. Horses will all need baths and liniment rubdowns when we get home. I'll be right back. Going to get Napoleon. Let's get this show on the road."

24

NAPOLEON

IT WAS A LITTLE AFTER THREE IN the afternoon when I led Napoleon inside the main barn at Oak Lane Stable. He'd been turned out in one of the grassy paddocks out back. It had been two days since the Shady Creek Stable's schooling show, and Stan had wanted the horses to have some time off after the show. I finally got to ride Napoleon today. Dad was coming in about twenty minutes to meet with Stan and watch me ride, which gave me some time to clean him up and then lunge him before I got on. At the moment, I had the barn to myself, except for a few of the boarders' horses who were in their stalls down at the other end of the aisle. I hadn't seen or heard from Ingrid since the show.

Earlier, Allison had tacked up Diamond Jack, Joe did Night Hawk, Mrs. Wagner cleaned up Snowdrops, and Claire finished up with Gallant Star. They had all decided to ride their horses outside along the pathway next to the cross-country course. The group had led their horses outside.

"We'll take it easy, mostly walking and some trotting," Claire had said. "The horses had a lot of work on Sunday, except for Snowdrops. Let's give them a chance to enjoy something other than ring work. Mrs. Wagner, you'll be able to see what Snowdrops is like outside. It's a good idea to try a horse in different settings before you buy them—to see how they handle things."

They all took turns mounting up and rode off toward the big field, talking among themselves until I couldn't hear them anymore. I had wanted to ride Gallant Star, but I had to try out Napoleon instead.

Napoleon clomped along beside me on the concrete aisle as I led him to the second pair of cross-ties in the barn, the ones across from Diamond Jack's stall. I clipped the cross-tie metal clasps onto his halter rings and went to get the grooming tools from the boarders' tack room. He sneezed twice.

After I brought the grooming box out and put it on the floor near me, I picked out the black rubber curry comb and started to rub Napoleon's golden chestnut coat in circles. Dust and shedding hair collected under the curry comb as I made my way over his left side of his body. A truck or a car with a rumbly exhaust pulled up outside the barn entrance by the time I made it to the top of his rump.

Two doors slammed.

Two men, talking loudly, walked in through the open barn doors.

I froze.

Elvis Chops smoked a cigarette as he turned to his right and looked into all of the stalls on his left down the show horses' aisle. Hippie Hair trailed along behind him and looked in at all of the stalls on his right. They both wore the same clothes they had had on at Shady Creek Stable's schooling show.

"See him?" Elvis Chops asked. He took a drag on his cigarette.

"Nah, he ain't in any of these stalls," Hippie Hair said.

"You're ... you're not supposed ... to smoke in the barn." I stepped closer to Napoleon's head. I held the curry comb in front of my chest with my arms pressed hard against my sides. My heart thudded like crazy.

They had already made it down to the end of the barn and were headed back toward me. I looked around quickly to see if anyone else was coming into the barn.

"Maybe he's turned out." Elvis Chops looked right at me and took another drag on his cigarette.

"Stan said ... no one is to smoke ... in the barn. What ... what do you want?" My legs felt like Jell-O water. I put my sweaty right palm against Napoleon's neck to hold onto something.

Elvis Chops walked right past me. He looked in the stalls on my left side and down to the other end of the barn. Hippie Hair looked at all of the stalls on the opposite side of Elvis Chops.

"What ... do ... you want?" I stood with my back toward Napoleon's shoulder. "Stan will be right here. Are ... are you looking for a horse?" My lower lip quivered. I wished Stan would hurry up and get back from Mrs. O'Mally's house. He had gone to talk to her about Night Hawk's training. He had said he'd only be gone a few minutes.

Please, please, please come back now, Stan!

"Yeah, that's it. We wanna buy a horse," Elvis Chops said.

Hippie Hair giggled like a girl. "Maybe get it for a steal."

Elvis Chops stopped right next to me, took another drag from his cigarette, and blew the smoke toward me. He shot out his hand and grabbed my left arm. "Where's the horse, kid?"

My eyes teared up. My stomach felt super-duper-flippy. It felt like I had to pee!

Dad, where are you?!

"Which … horse?"

Napoleon snorted. He shifted his weight and rocked back and forth. His ears went back. The whites of his eyes showed. He snorted again.

"Yeah, where's the horse?" Hippie Hair said as he stood next to Elvis Chops.

"I don't know … what horse are you talking about?" My arm hurt where he gripped it.

"That jumper one," Elvis Chops leaned in and squeezed my arm even harder. I dropped the black rubber curry comb.

"There are … a lot of … jumpers here." I tried to back up against Napoleon some more, but he still danced around.

Elvis Chops shoved me hard and backwards when he let go of my arm. Napoleon tried to move away from me when I landed against him. The cross-ties kept him from bolting.

"Hey, man, that horse ain't here. Let's beat it." Elvis Chops turned and walked toward the barn door.

"Yeah, let's beat it," Hippie Hair said as he followed along.

I held my arm where Elvis Chops had gripped it and then tried to calm Napoleon down. He still danced around and pulled back against the cross-ties.

What did they want?

Elvis Chops took a last drag on his cigarette and flicked it toward the barn's office door. He laughed as they left the barn.

I stared at the spot where the cigarette had landed. I tried to walk over on rubbery legs to crush out the cigarette. Their noisy engine started and the tires squealed as their vehicle peeled away from the barn's parking lot.

When I thought it was safe, I took the cigarette butt outside. I wanted to hose it down to make sure it was soaked. I could hardly turn the water spicket on, my hands trembled like crazy. I left the soggy butt on the driveway. I had most of the green garden hose wound up again when Dad pulled in and parked his car in the first spot by the main barn.

"Dad!" I dropped the hose and ran over to him. I started to cry like a baby before I even grabbed onto him and hugged him around his waist. I made tight fists where I held onto the back of his light-blue T-shirt. I buried my face against his chest. My shoulders shook like crazy. I couldn't make them stop.

"Cassie, what's wrong?" Dad asked me. He held me tightly and pressed me against him. "Did you get hurt? Hey, it's okay. I'm here." He just let me cry and hold him until I finally stopped. The front of his T-shirt was pretty soggy where I had held my face against him.

"What happened?" Dad asked.

"There were these two guys from the horse show ... I saw them there first ... and then they were here ... and then the one guy, Elvis Chops, was smoking in the barn." I wiped snot off from under my nose with the back of my right wrist and rubbed it off on the bottom of my purple T-shirt.

"Hey, slow down," Dad said. "I can't understand you when you talk so fast. Stan, something upset Cass."

Stan had walked up to us. "Did Napoleon hurt you?"

"No, ... Oh, Napoleon!" I turned to go back into the barn. "They spooked him, too!"

"Who spooked Napoleon?" Stan followed behind me.

"She said something about two guys being here." Dad walked beside Stan.

Napoleon stood on the cross-ties and pawed the aisle floor with his left front hoof. He flipped up his head and whinnied when we approached him.

"Easy, boy," I said as I grabbed onto the cross-tie and ran my hand down his damp, sweaty neck. "Easy now."

"From the top, Cassie, tell us what happened," Dad said.

"There were these two creepy guys I saw at the Shady Lane Stable schooling show. They were really mean to me. Made me drop my hot dog. The one guy I call Elvis Chops—because his sideburns look like Elvis'—smoked and blew it in my face. He threw his cigarette at Shady Lane Stable's main barn, and I had to put it out. They just laughed." I ran my hand over Napoleon's shoulder until he calmed down.

"What happened today?" Stan asked as he squinted and crossed his arms.

"They were just here and walked through the barn looking for something. I think they were looking for a horse. They kept asking each other if they saw the horse. I …I tried to find out what they wanted. I told them you'd be right back, Stan. The one guy grabbed my arm and … and Elvis Chops smoked while he was in here. He threw his burning cigarette at the office! They were mean to me again. And they spooked Napoleon."

"Who grabbed your arm?" Dad looked me over for bruises.

I looked down at my boot toes. "Elvis Chops did. I tried not to be scared, but—"

"Don't like this." Stan squinted harder and rubbed his chin with his left hand. "No, sir, don't like this one bit. Better make a call. You can wait until tomorrow to ride Napoleon, if you want."

"Maybe you should wait." Dad leaned over toward me.

"No, I'm okay." I went over to pick up a brush to run it over Napoleon's body. "And Napoleon has calmed down. My arm is a little sore, that's all."

"Let's not expect too much. Join you in the ring when I'm done making this call." Stan headed toward his office.

"I'll come with you, Stan," Dad said as he turned to catch up to Stan. "No one lays a hand on my daughter. I want to know what's going on here." They both walked together to the office and disappeared inside.

I finished grooming Napoleon and tacked him up. I got the lunge line, clipped it onto his bridle, and walked him into the indoor. I led him to the right side of the ring where there weren't any jumps and asked him to walk in a circle around me the length of the nylon lunge line. He listened fine.

"Trot." I clucked to him to get him to move faster. He picked up a working trot. I let him go around me a few times. "Canter." I flipped the long lunge whip. It cracked a bit. Napoleon started out cantering smooth and collected, but suddenly gained speed.

"Whoa, Napoleon!" I pulled back on the lunge line to try and slow him down. All he did was pick up more speed. He dragged me across the ring as he sped around me in big circles. He kept getting faster and faster and faster!

"Whoa! Whoa, Napoleon! I said whoa!" I dropped the lunge whip and held onto the lunge line with both hands.

He pulled hard against me. He whinnied and bucked and ran fast circles around me.

"Cassie, get him under control!" Stan shouted. He and Dad had come into the ring.

"I'm trying to," I pulled back against Napoleon, "but he's too strong!"

Stan timed it just right as he ran up to me and grabbed onto the lunge line. "Whoa, now. Easy ... that's right ... easy boy ... good boy." We made a few circles together.

Napoleon slowed down to a trot and then walked. His sides puffed and his nostrils were huge. He was covered in dark sweat. My saddle had slid back.

"Whoa," Stan pulled in the extra length of the lunge line as Napoleon walked in and stopped in front of us. "Now that he's plenty warmed up, let's fix your saddle, and you can get on him." He loosened the girth, lifted the saddle and pad forward, reached under his belly, and rebuckled the girth under the saddle flap. He pulled down my stirrup irons, tightened the girth one more time, and gave me a leg up.

"Walk him a bit, then pick up a posting trot," Stan said.

"Is he all right?" Dad stood with us in the ring. "He's not too strong for her, is he?"

"Don't know yet." Stan patted Napoleon's wet neck. "We're not off to a good start, but it might just be from getting rattled earlier."

"I don't want her getting hurt." Dad crossed his arms to watch. "Her mother would have my head if she did."

I nudged Napoleon with my heels and rode him to the rail. I let him walk on a loose rein so he could have his head. He felt big and solid beneath me. I sat on him differently than I did on George or Snowdrops or even Gallant Star. Napoleon was taller than the other horses at 16.2 hands and solid muscle.

Why was he acting so strong? Would I be able to control him? Maybe he was better off with a more experienced rider on his back.

"Okay, let him trot," Stan said.

I shortened my reins a bit, clucked at him, and squeezed with both of my lower legs. He immediately picked up an even trot. I hardly had to work at posting because his gait was so smooth.

"How come every other horse I ride is easier than George?" I used the whole ring by riding in both directions, working in and around the jumps.

"Old George was flashy when he was young. You'd be tired, too, if you had as many miles on you as he does." Stan smiled at me after I rode past him and Dad. "Let's canter."

I brought Napoleon down to a walk. I squeezed my right rein, pressed my right lower leg against his side, and pushed down in my seat bones. Napoleon easily picked up his left canter lead. I rocked gently to his 3-beat gait. He covered ground faster than any other horse I'd ever ridden before. The ring went by almost in a blur. I had to watch where I was going.

What would he be like if he had room to run?

"Switch directions." Stan walked over to the jump area and adjusted two fences so they were about 2-foot, 6-inches high.

"Looks good, Cass." Dad stood by Stan.

I asked Napoleon to do a flying change of lead, and he actually did it!

Napoleon had picked up speed. I squeezed my fingers on the reins to slow him. He responded a bit, but not as much as I wanted him to.

"Ride him down the line here," Stan said. "Keep moving him forward. That's it, nice and steady. Not so fast."

I swung Napoleon toward the first fence—a two-pole vertical—and he pricked up his ears.

"Whoa, easy boy." I tightened my fingers on the reins as we approached the fence.

I sat deeper in the seat and waited until he left the ground. Wow! He jumped big and round. I got left behind in the saddle and landed without my right stirrup iron. I had to grab onto his mane to stay on. Napoleon picked up more speed as he approached the next fence.

"Cassie, sit up and take your reins now!" Stan shouted at me.

"He jumps so big! I lost my stirrup!" I barely managed to hang on as Napoleon flew over the second fence. Napoleon bucked when he got over the fence. I lost my balance, although I had never regained it after going over the first fence, and tried to hang on but got dumped off after he bucked three more times. He squealed with each buck. I hit the dirt and rolled to a stop. Napoleon ran over to the other side of the ring where he had gone crazy when I tried to lunge him earlier.

"Cassie! Are you all right?" Dad was by my side in an instant. He helped get me to my feet. "Are you hurt?"

"No, I don't think so." I brushed off my butt. I spit out some dirt. Dad brushed off my back.

"Sure you're okay?" Stan led Napoleon over to us after he caught him.

"I'm fine," I lied. My left arm hurt. I brushed off my knees with my right hand.

"Good, I'll give you a leg up," Stan said.

"I—"

"This time, hang on." Stan put out his right hand to give me a leg up. He easily hoisted me onto Napoleon's back.

I picked up the reins and took a breath. My stomach was flippy. I knew I had to try again. I turned Napoleon toward the rail and asked him to pick up a canter. He rocked along smoothly.

"Come down the line." Stan stood with his arms crossed.

I came out of the corner and headed toward the fence. My fingers gripped the reins. My left arm ached. I squeezed my knees tighter. I sat back and pushed my heels down deeper. Napoleon kept a steady pace and jumped the first fence. We cantered to the second fence, took that fence in stride, and cantered in a large circle before I asked him to halt. I let out my breath. I patted Napoleon's shoulder.

"Much better," Stan said. "He jumps big, but you did a great job. Let him walk now. Both of you've had enough for one day."

I let the reins out, and Napoleon dropped his head to walk around the ring.

"What do you think?" Dad asked Stan. He rubbed his chin. "I thought you said he'd be a good horse for Cass."

"Not sure," Stan said. "Luke said his rider doesn't have a problem with him. Seems too strong for my taste. Don't want Cassie losing her confidence or, worse, getting hurt."

"I don't either," Dad said. "Cass, what do you think?"

"He's strong, but maybe with some work I'd learn to ride him better." I let Napoleon walk near them.

Dad rubbed his chin with his hand. "I don't know—"

"Could try him again tomorrow and see how he goes. He's in a new environment and got all worked up today." Stan scratched the back of his neck.

"You'll have to ride tomorrow after supper." Dad looked up at me. "I had a half day of vacation today. Your mom can watch then too."

"I'll make sure Napoleon spends the day outside so he can work off some of that energy before you come. Don't want a repeat of today." Stan turned to face Dad.

"Neither do I," Dad said.

"Do you want me to give him a liniment bath?" I asked Stan. I pulled up Napoleon near them. Maybe I'd rub some liniment on my arm to help it from hurting. "He sure got a workout today."

"Wouldn't be a bad idea. Make sure the water is warm." Stan reached up and patted Napoleon's neck.

I took my feet out of the stirrup irons, wiggled my ankles, and slid down. I loosened the girth, ran up my stirrups, and followed Stan and Dad as they walked out of the ring. I gently rubbed my left arm where Elvis Chops had grabbed me. I kicked at the dirt with my right foot.

If I couldn't ride and stay on Napoleon over fences that weren't even three feet high, how would I ever ride Gallant Star over a jumper course?

What a super-crummy day.

25
NAPOLEON HEADS HOME

I SQUATTED DOWN ON THE BARN floor and wrapped Napoleon's left front leg with the quilted shipping wraps that were used to protect the horses' legs when they traveled, especially over long distances. I pinned the gray bandage overlay to secure it, and then got up, grabbed another set of bandages from the floor, knelt down, and started to wrap his other front leg. I still had to wrap his hind legs.

Napoleon was going back to his owner's stable near Libertyville, Illinois this morning. He would ride in the horse van along with Gallant Star and Oak Lane Stable's four other jumpers who were entered in an A-rated horse show in Libertyville.

"Whoa, Napoleon," I said. He shifted his weight when I tried to wrap his left hind leg. "Easy now. It's okay."

"I'll hold him for you," Stan said after he walked up to us. He held the cross-tie by Napoleon's halter and stroked Napoleon's neck. "Keith has Gallant Star wrapped and is finishing up with Night Hawk. We'll load the show trunks first and then the horses."

I had ridden Napoleon a few more times during the two weeks he had been at Oak Lane Stable, but each time I rode him he was just too strong for me. He bucked me off three more times. Stan and Dad had gotten mad. I had thought they were mad at me because I couldn't control Napoleon, but Stan had said, "Cassie, it isn't your fault. Luke should have been honest with me about how much work Napoleon needed before he could be ridden, especially for a young rider."

I had actually been glad to ride George instead of Napoleon for my lessons. At least I knew I could stay on him, most of the time. Stan even let me ride Gallant Star a few times. I think Stan felt bad for having Napoleon come to the barn for me to try in the first place.

"I'm almost done. I just have to wrap this last leg." I knelt down to finish with his right hind leg.

"Sorry things didn't work out with Napoleon." Stan kept a firm hand on the cross-tie and ran his hand down Napoleon's nose. "Sometimes you can't get the run out of a horse that's been on the track. He might settle down when he gets older, but then, maybe not either. He's a big beautiful horse, but you need a horse who will take better care of you, someone who is more sensible and wants to do what you ask rather than plowing around the ring and acting like a crazy horse."

"It's okay." I stood up and brushed my knees off. "He's a lot of horse for me, at least right now. Dad said I have to wait to get a better one for me."

"Don't worry, we'll find the perfect one for you." Stan let go of the cross-tie.

When?

"Keith has all of the horses wrapped now," Stan said as he looked down at his wrist watch. "Only about a two-hour drive for us. Luke said he'd meet us at the showgrounds around 11 o'clock to pick up Napoleon. Should make it in plenty of time. Keep Napoleon on the cross-ties. It'll be only a few minutes before we load up." Stan turned to walk away.

"Do you think Gallant Star will win his jumper classes at this show?" I walked up by Napoleon's head and held onto the cross-tie.

"Don't know, Cassie," Stan said. "It's an A-rated show. He'll be up against some tough competition. Did great at Shady Creek Stable, but we'll see how he handles a professional show and go from there."

"I know he can win," I said.

"Hope so," Stan said. "He's turned into a nice horse. He deserves a shot at the big time."

"I can't wait to watch him on Saturday afternoon in the Open Jumper Class." I followed Stan to the other side of the barn. "I'm going to wish him luck since I won't get to see him for a few days."

"Let you know when we're ready for Napoleon," Stan said. "Keith, let's get the trunks loaded first." He walked into the boarders' tack room to help Keith with the equipment.

I opened Gallant Star's stall door and went inside. Gallant Star turned from eating his hay and nickered softly to me. His coat shone like deep red glass and his black mane and tail looked silky smooth. His shipping wraps were neat and tight.

"Hi, boy." I let him sniff my left palm. The warm breath from his nostrils snuffed softly across my hand. I ran my hand over his warm velvety neck and then moved in closer to press my cheek against his strong shoulder. "Now, you're going to a big show. You might be nervous. I get nervous, too, but you'll do fine. Just show them how wonderful you are. Maybe Dad will finally buy you for me then."

Gallant Star turned his head toward me when I wrapped my arms around his neck.

I whispered, "I love you, Gallant Star."

"Cassie, we're ready for Napoleon." Stan called out to me from inside the open barn doors.

"Be good," I said to Gallant Star. "I'll see you in four days." I gave him a final pat on his neck, slipped out of his stall, and then went to get Napoleon for Stan to load into the horse van.

26

GALLANT STAR AT LIBERTYVILLE

STAN DROVE THE STABLE'S OLD truck onto the horse show grounds around 11:45 Saturday morning and pulled into an empty spot near the stabling area in the back parking lot. It was really more like a big field where the riders and trainers parked their vehicles, horse trailers, and big horse vans for the five days of the Libertyville Horse Show.

"There sure are a lot of people here." I pushed open my squeaky truck door. "Look at how many horse trailers and vans are parked here."

"This kind of show will always bring in a lot of competition." Stan slammed his door shut and then grabbed two bridles, a white saddle pad, and three dark blue towels from the truck's rusted rear cargo trunk. "Horse shows near Chicago usually are busy."

"Can I carry something?" I asked.

Stan smiled and handed me the towels. "Here."

"I can't wait to see Gallant Star go in his class later today. I told you he'd win." I adjusted the towels in my arms as we walked into Oak Lane Stable's show area. Keith had Night Hawk on cross-ties and was brushing out his tail.

"Yes, you did." Stan put down the bridles and saddle pad on one of the show trunks that were set up in the aisle. "Was first rate in both of his first two classes. Told Joe not to overdo it with him, just let Gallant Star feel things out. He beat the other horses easily."

"Hi, Keith," I said. "Where do you want the towels, Stan?"

"Put them in the trunk you're standing in front of," Keith answered for Stan.

"Okay." I opened the lid, put the towels in the bottom, and closed it back up.

"Gallant Star is attracting a lot of attention from the other riders and trainers." Stan crossed his arms. "Had two guys come up to me after Gallant Star won his second class. Asked a lot of questions, like where I bought him, how long I've had him, things like that. Didn't care much for those two. Told them we had work to do and headed off for the stable. Haven't seen them since."

Two guys? Like two creepy guys?

"Hey, I had two guys in here yesterday morning nosing around the horses in their stalls," Keith said. "One guy smoked a cigarette. I told him to put it out or go outside. The guy acted all tough. All I did was walk toward him, and he backed off. They walked away."

One guy smoked a cigarette?

"Let's keep an eye on things," Stan said.

"Will do," Keith said.

"Where's Gallant Star's stall?" I asked. My stomach felt flippy-floppy.

"Right here." Stan stood in front of the fourth stall along the wall of the barn. It was to the right of an open doorway that was in the middle of the barn wall and also led outside to the back parking lot where Stan had parked the truck.

I walked up to Stan and looked in through the iron stall bars. Gallant Star came over to us. I opened the bolt on the stall door and went inside. "Hi, boy. How are you?" I ran my hand over his neck. He seemed happy to see me.

"He was excited at first when we got here, but settled down quickly," Stan said. "Looks extra fine when he goes toward the show ring like he did at Shady Creek Stable's show."

"He's beautiful," I said.

"He should be. I rubbed on him for over a half an hour to get his coat shiny for the class." Keith came over by us.

"All the horses groomed?" Stan asked Keith.

"Yup," Keith said. "Everybody's ready to go."

"Let's get lunch before the class starts." Stan looked at his watch. "We've got about an hour before we need to start. Night Hawk and Gallant Star don't go until later in the class, but the two other jumpers we brought will go earlier. Besides, Cassie, I promised your dad that I wouldn't let you starve. Come on."

Keith put Night Hawk into his stall, and I bolted Gallant Star's stall door behind me. The three of us walked out of the barn. Stan steered us toward the community building near the main outdoor show ring where long lines of people were already waiting to order something to eat. I could smell hamburgers before we even got to the small white building. I was hungrier than I thought.

27
Horse Thieves Try Again

I FINISHED EATING MY HAMBURGER with ketchup only and a bag of potato chips as I stood near the food stand. Stan and Keith ate their lunches around a tall wooden table that you could only stand at. The whole area was crowded with trainers and riders. Everyone talked to each other while they ate their food.

"Anyone interested in walking the jumper course may do so now before the class begins," a man announced over the loudspeakers.

"I'd better find Joe," Stan said as he crumpled his white paper napkin. "I think he's already by the ring. I saw him walking down there a few minutes ago."

"I see Jody, Napoleon's groom," Keith said. "I have something I need to talk to him about. I'll be only a few minutes." He made his way through the crowd to find his friend.

"I want to go back to the barn," I said to Stan. "I'll meet you there." I held onto my paper cup of orange soda and started toward our stable area.

"Oh, Stan ... Stan, I have someone I want you to meet," a woman I'd never seen before touched Stan's arm to hold him back. "This is Mr. And Mrs. Jonathon Edwards. They want to talk to you about ..."

I let Stan have his grown-up talk. I walked back to the barn. Before I even put my soda down on the show trunk near Gallant Star's stall I smelled them—cigarettes.

The hair on my arms and under the back of my braid felt all frizzly again like at Shady Creek Stable's show.

Gallant Star's stall door was wide open.

"Gallant Star?" I poked my head inside.

Empty.

Straw had been dragged out of the stall and onto the barn aisle in front of Gallant Star's door.

Had Keith beaten me to the barn? He said he was going to talk to Jody. Even if he hadn't found Jody, would he have made it back to the barn before I did? Did Joe take Gallant Star somewhere?

I looked out the barn door I had just come in and scanned the area toward the showring. Trainers and riders were walking the course. The only horses I saw were being ridden in the warm-up ring on the other side of the main ring where the jumper class was to be held.

No Gallant Star.

I turned and went back inside the barn. I looked up and down the aisles to see if maybe he had gotten out of his stall on his own, but there were only horses on cross-ties being brushed by their grooms.

Still no Gallant Star.

I walked to the open barn door that separated the stalls in our show aisle—the one next to Gallant Star's stall. I went outside and again scanned the area. I walked down a small hill and out into the big parking lot where Stan had parked the truck and tried to see if he was loose out there and eating grass. I didn't see him.

I turned around to walk back to the barn, but stopped when I heard men shouting in the distance. I followed the parking lot driveway in the direction I had heard the noise. After hearing the men shout a few more times, I knew I was going in the right direction.

Then I froze.

Elvis Chops and Hippie Hair had Gallant Star! They were trying to load him into a rusty two-horse trailer hooked up to a beat-up farm truck. The trailer's ramp was down and Gallant Star fought them every time the guys tried to get him loaded up on the ramp.

"Hurry up! Get him in there!" Elvis Chops pulled on the rope that was attached to Gallant Star's halter as he shouted at Hippie Hair.

"He won't budge!" Hippie Hair shouted back. "He keeps jumping the ramp."

They kept trying to pull Gallant Star onto the ramp, but he reared up and struck out his front legs at Hippie Hair.

"Hey, man, get him away from me!" Hippie Hair screamed.

"Pull on your rope!" Elvis Chops yelled. He backed away from Gallant Star's flying hooves.

I made fists and ran as fast as I could toward them. I screamed, "LET GO OF MY HORSE!!!"

Their heads shot around to face me.

"LET GO OF HIM!" I screamed again as I raced up to them.

They looked at each other and hesitated. Then they turned away and tried to load Gallant Star again.

"Beat it, kid!" Elvis Chops shouted at me, then turned to Hippie Hair. "Pull on your rope, and get him in!"

"Man, he won't get in!" Hippie Hair shouted back.

"LET GO!" I grabbed hard onto Elvis Chops' arm that held the rope attached to Gallant Star's halter. "He's NOT your horse!"

Fighter-fast, Elvis Chops jerked his arm away from mine, grabbed my shoulder, and shoved me down on the gravel driveway. "Last time, kid, beat it, or you'll get what's coming to you!" he yelled down at me and kicked me hard—twice.

"Oww!" I scrambled to get away. Bloody scrapes from the sharp driveway gravel ran down my arms and palms. My right wrist hurt from trying to catch myself before I had hit the ground.

"Get him in the trailer now, or you'll get some of that, too!" Elvis Chops yelled at Hippie Hair.

I ran away while they still tried to force Gallant Star into the two-horse trailer. Gallant Star continued to run over the ramp, pull back, and rear to keep from going in. His neck was wet and sweat lathered between his hind legs. He whinny-screamed a few times.

I shot back toward the barn. I bolted inside our aisle, but didn't see Keith.

Why wasn't he back already?

Stan was down at the ring. I hoped I could find him and Joe. I didn't think they had finished walking the course yet.

I raced down to the main ring, trying to avoid the trainers and riders who were making their way there. Stan was still talking to the same women who had stopped him on the way back to the barn after lunch. There was another couple with them. Joe stood next to Stan.

My chest heaved. My lungs burned. I grabbed his arm. "Stan ... Stan ... I—"

"Cassie! What's wrong?" Stan took a hold of my arms.

I could barely get it out. "They're ... trying ... to ... steal—"

"Steal? What?" A man standing next to Stan asked.

My chest finally stopped heaving. "Gallant ... those two guys ... trying to steal him—"

"Goodness, is someone trying to steal my Rocky again?" said the woman who stood next to the man I didn't know. She held a rolled up magazine in her hand.

Her Rocky?

"In the back parking lot." I pointed in that direction.

"Mrs. Edwards, get security," Stan said. "Tell them to meet us in the back parking lot by the east entrance. Joe, find Keith. Tell him to meet us back there. Jonathon, let's see what we can do. Cassie, show us where they are."

Stan, the Jonathon-man, and I raced back to the parking lot.

Thank goodness Elvis Chops and Hippie Hair hadn't been able to load Gallant Star. He still fought the two men, but I could tell he was getting tired. He was soaked in sweat and lather and wasn't dancing around as hard as he had before.

"LET GO OF MY HORSE!" the Jonathon-man shouted. He ran pretty fast for an old guy.

"STOP!" Stan yelled as he charged at the thieves.

Gallant Star let out a giant whinny scream.

"Let go, you creeps!" I kept back, though.

"Oh, man, let's get out of here!" Hippie Hair screamed at Elvis Chops. He let go of his end of the rope.

"Move it, man!" Elvis Chops yelled back. He let go of his end of the rope and ran for the truck door.

Gallant Star jumped back and away from the trailer. He dragged the long ropes along behind him.

Both thieves dove into the truck, started the noisy engine, and gunned it down the driveway. Gravel flew out from the truck's tires, dragging the trailer ramp they never had time to close. They swerved as they made their way down the long driveway and out of the entrance gate. The truck and trailer sped down the road and out of sight.

"Won't get far with that trailer ramp dragging behind them," Stan said. "A sheriff's deputy is on his way and will pull them over soon enough."

The Jonathon-man walked Gallant Star up to Stan and me. He had caught Gallant Star after the thieves had dropped their ropes and made a run for it. Gallant Star was still puffing through his nostrils. He was covered in sweat.

"Do you want me to take Gallant Star and walk him?" I asked Stan.

"No, Cassie, we'll let Mr. Edwards walk his horse," Stan said.

His horse?

I frowned.

"Is he all right?" the woman who Stan had told to get security and who still held the rolled-up magazine still in her hand quickly approached us. "They didn't hurt him, did they? They didn't hurt my Rocky Baby."

Her Rocky Baby? What was she talking about?

"No, dear, he looks fine, just some sweat on him that's easily washed off. Other than that, he looks great. Stan, you did a marvelous job keeping him fit while you cared for him," the Jonathon-man said while he gave Gallant Star a solid pat on his wet neck.

"Oh, I never thought I'd see you again, Rocky." The woman went up to Gallant Star and ran her hand gently down his nose. He then rubbed his head against her. "I thought you were gone for good."

"Gone for good?" I asked.

Stan said, "Cassie, this is Mr. And Mrs. Jonathon Edwards—"

"Call me, Helen," the woman by Gallant Star said. "Nice to meet you, Cassie."

"Jonathon and Helen Edwards are Gallant Star's owners," Stan said. "His real name is Sky Rocket, the champion show jumper. They've been looking for him for almost eight months."

"We had him shipped from the East Coast to our stable outside of Chicago after the final shows." Jonathon Edwards wiped some sweat off of Gallant Star's neck. "He never came home. He went missing when we used a different horse shipper than our regular one. Rocky ended up being stolen, maybe by those two who just tried to take him now."

"Stan told us the story of Rocky being rescued," Helen Edwards said. "Thank goodness he was saved in time, both times! I hated to think something awful had happened to him. We'll be forever grateful to you, Stan."

I wanted to keep Gallant Star. "Maybe this isn't your—"

"Cassie," Stan said.

Helen Edwards walked up to me. "Here's a magazine article about Rocky and us. See? We're right here." She opened the magazine, the same issue that Stan let me read back in June. She showed me the photos that Allison, Ingrid, and I had looked at back then.

"We also breed our own horses, and each foal is branded in a small spot right under the mane, on the neck. Here, let me show you." She walked over to Gallant Star's right side and lifted his mane. She motioned for me to come over by her.

I walked over. She showed me a small white swirl mark under his mane and near the top crest of his neck. I hadn't noticed it before. My heart felt heavy. My shoulders drooped.

"I thought his star was smaller when we first had him," Stan said. "Took Polaroids of him to watch his recovery and thought his star kept getting bigger each month. Thieves must have used hair dye to color it out."

"He has white coronet bands above both of his hind hooves," Jonathon Edwards said. "I'll bet once we clip off that black dyed hair we'll see his white marks. If you look closely, his hooves show signs of being pink feet and not gray ones under that awful black hoof polish, which will eventually wear off. I'd better walk him around to cool him down a bit."

"I can do that for you." I reached for Gallant Star's ropes.

"Thank you for offering, young lady," Jonathon Edwards said, "but I think I'll hang onto him now that he's back in my possession. Helen, let's take him to our neighbor's stable area until we can get our stable van here. Wait until the others see who's come home!"

"Home?" I asked. "You mean—"

"Yes, Cassie, the Edwards are taking him home," Stan said.

My throat got all lumpy again. "But, shouldn't we—"

"Thank you so much for all that you've done for us," Jonathon Edwards said. "We'll come back later to talk some more. We have so much more to learn about Rocky's time with you."

"I ... I have to say good-bye?" I asked. Tears welled up.

I was not going to cry like a baby in front of them.

"I'm afraid so," Stan said. "Gallant St—I mean, Sky Rocket, needs to be with his rightful owners."

"You can come and see him anytime, dear," Helen Edwards said. "I'm sure he'd like that."

I walked over to Gallant Star, or Sky Rocket, or whatever they wanted to call him, and wrapped my arms around his still-wet neck. I didn't care. I held onto him as tightly as I could. "Good-bye, Gallant Star." He turned his head toward me and nuzzled my side. I held him tighter. I pressed my face against his damp coat.

"We still have a jumper class to compete in," Stan said.

I let go and gave Gallant Star a final pat on the neck.

All of us walked up to the barn and in through the open door next to where Gallant Star's stall had been for the show. I watched as the Edwards led Gallant Star away down through the barn aisle and then disappeared among the show crowd. Stan talked to Joe and Keith about what had happened.

I turned, went back outside through the barn door we had just come in, and cried.

28
MISERY LOVES COMPANY

DEXTER CURLED UP NEXT TO ME on my twin bed and purred while I stroked his black fur. He reached out his right white paw and put it on my chest. I hadn't been to the barn in over two weeks.

I looked up at the framed posters of the jumping horses mounted on the bedroom walls. All of the ribbons I had won at horse shows since I was a little kid hung in a single row along the top of the longest bedroom wall. Dad had helped me to hang them up. I had hoped I could win enough ribbons to go all the way around the room. The first-place ribbon I had won with George at Shady Creek Stable hung above my bedroom desk.

"You can stay here." I pushed myself up and let Dexter sit in the warm spot I had made on the bed. He curled up against the pillow and licked his fur.

I went over to my collection of plastic horse statues. They had a bookcase all to themselves next to my desk. I picked up my bay horse statue, Justin Morgan. I put him back on the shelf and moved around my Clydesdale and Palomino statues so they could make friends with the Arabian and Tennessee Walker statues.

Maybe horse statues were for babies.

I sat down at my desk and straightened the pile of new notebooks and folders Mom had gotten for me. School started next week. A purple plastic pencil case rested against the pile of folders. I opened it up and dug through the unsharpened #2 pencils and the new ballpoint pens. I zipped the case shut and tossed it back by the folder pile. My arms dropped to my sides. I stared at the desktop.

Then, I opened the desk drawer. I took out a flat rectangular piece of brass. It felt cool in my hands. I kept it in the desk drawer since it was too long to fit into my box of special treasures. I ran my right fingers over the name etched in dark blue. Stan had given it to me after we had gotten back to Oak Lane Stable from the Libertyville horse show while I had waited for Mom to pick me up.

"Would you like to have this?" Stan had asked me after he had slid out Gallant Star's nameplate from his stall door and offered it to me.

I had nodded. My throat had been lumpy, like it was now. Stan had put his hand on my shoulder when I took it. After Mom and I had gotten home, I went directly to my bedroom, curled up on my bed, and held the nameplate against my heart. I cried like crazy. I couldn't stop. I hadn't been to the barn since.

"I don't even want a horse anymore," I said to Dexter, who stopped cleaning his fur when I looked over at him. He squinted up at me and went back to his cat bath.

"Why do things have to be so super-rotten?" I grabbed two pieces of tissue from the box on my desk, blew my nose, and threw the snotty mess into the wicker trash can next to my desk. The tissues joined the other tissues from the past few days. It was getting pretty full.

"Cassie?" Mom called out as she came to the top of the stairs.

I slipped Gallant Star's nameplate inside the desk drawer.

"You ARE in here," Mom said as she came into my room. She walked up to me and put her hand on my shoulder. "Your dad and I are going over to the barn to give Stan a check. Would you like to ride along?"

"Do I have to?" I put my hands in my lap.

"No, you don't have to, but you haven't left your room much or seen Allison and Ingrid in a while. Don't you want a change of scenery?" Mom looked down at me and smiled.

"No, I'm fine here," I said. "Can't you just send the check? I don't know how much riding I'm going to do anymore anyway. School starts next week, and I'll probably have lots of homework and ... " I looked up at her.

"Come with us. It'll do you some good." Mom placed her right fingers under my chin.

"No, I'm—"

"Cassandra," Mom said.

"Okay, but only because you're making me go." I pushed the chair back to get up.

"Meet your father and me in the car in five minutes." Mom turned and walked out of the room. She went downstairs.

"Great," I said to Dexter when I sat on the bed by him. "Why can't I just stay here with you? You'd like that, wouldn't you?" I scratched his favorite spot under his chin.

Dexter squinted and purred.

"Cassie!" Mom called up from the bottom of the stairway.

"Coming!" I gave Dexter one last scratch, slid off the bed, and headed toward the bedroom door.

29

THE BIGGEST SURPRISE OF ALL

WHEN WE GOT TO OAK LANE STABLE, Dad pulled into the second parking spot by the barn doors right next to Grandma Leona's red Cadillac Eldorado with its white vinyl roof.

"Why is Grandma Leona here?" I waited for Mom to open the car door so she could get out, tip the front seat forward, and let me out of the backseat.

"Is that your mother's car?" Dad asked Mom. The two of them smiled at each other over the top of the car.

Was Grandma Leona here?

"Let's find Stan and take him his check." Dad headed toward the open barn doors with a green bank check folded in half in his right hand. "I think he said to meet us in his office."

Dad and Mom walked into the barn.

I hung back and tried to come up with some excuse as to why I couldn't follow them in. I ran my right tennie toe back and forth in the grass. I wasn't at it long.

"Cassie, are you coming?" Mom came back and stood in the barn's doorway.

I stopped running my toe back and forth. "I just—"

"Come," Mom said and motioned for me to go inside.

I took a deep breath, let it out, and walked inside the barn.

Keith had Snowdrops on the first set of cross-ties on the boarders' side of the barn. He was probably cleaning her up for Mrs. Wagner so she could ride her when she got to the barn. He brushed her dappled coat with a soft body brush. Snowdrops stood patiently while he groomed her. She turned her head and softly nickered to us as we came into the barn. Thankfully, her body blocked the view to Gallant Star's empty stall.

I walked up to her and patted her neck. I didn't want to be able to see that empty stall.

"I'll find your father," Mom said as she headed toward Stan's office door. She went inside.

"Hi, Cassie," Keith said. "How are you doing?" He brushed Snowdrops' tail out until it was silky smooth.

"I ... I miss him." My throat got all tight up. I choked it back. I let Snowdrops nuzzle my left palm.

I wasn't going to cry in front of him.

"I know, it's tough. Gallant Star, or should I say, Sky Rocket, is a great horse, but he deserves to be with his real owners." Keith brushed out Snowdrops' mane.

"I know, but still—"

"The Edwards said you could visit him anytime." Keith tossed the mane brush back into the grooming box. "You can watch him at shows and cheer him on." He smiled at me.

"I suppose so, but when will we be at the same shows?" I pressed my face against Snowdrops' warm soft neck. Her coat smelled all horsey and wonderful. Mrs. Wagner was so lucky to be buying Snowdrops.

"Don't worry, you'll see him again," Keith said. "I'd bet on it."

The office door opened, and Stan, Dad, Mom, and Grandma Leona walked out. They came and stood next to us.

"You are here!" I said to Grandma Leona. I went over and hugged her. I instantly smelled like her powdery perfume. "I knew it was your car parked outside."

"Who said it wasn't?" Grandma Leona glanced at Mom and Dad. She gave me a tight hug.

"So, what do you think, Cassie?" Stan asked me.

"What do I think about what?" I asked. All four of them smiled at me. I turned toward Keith, and even he grinned like crazy.

"She doesn't know?" Stan asked Dad.

"No, not yet," Dad said.

Mom stood next to Dad.

"Know what?" I asked.

"How do you like your new horse?" Stan asked me.

I froze. I looked at all of their faces. I then looked around the barn and tried to think if any new horses had come into the barn before Gallant Star left. *Wouldn't Dad or Stan have told me if a new horse was coming in for me to try? No one said anything to me about that lately. Did a new horse come in the past two weeks when I wasn't here?*

"What new horse?"

"Cassie, dear," Grandma Leona put her arm around my shoulders and turned me to face Snowdrops, "this is your new horse."

"Snowdrops? But she's going to be Mrs. Wagner's new horse. I—"

"Mrs. Wagner decided not to buy her," Stan said. "Her daughter doesn't want to ride much anymore, so she passed on Snowdrops. Now, she's your horse."

"Snowdrops has always been the best horse for you," Dad said. "I know you wanted to have Gallant Star or Sky something—"

"Sky Rocket," Stan, Keith, and I said together.

"Okay, Sky Rocket, but Snowdrops is really more suited to your level of riding now. One day you'll ride a horse like Sky Rocket, but not until you get a few more years of riding experience." Dad walked over and patted Snowdrops' neck.

"But I thought she was too expensive." I felt numb. "Is this for real? Is she really my horse? You're not fooling, are you?"

"She's a gift from your dad, mom, and me," Grandma Leona said.

"I have a horse?" I just stood there.

"Yes," Dad said. He smiled at me.

I have a horse. I HAVE A HORSE!

"And, she's a beauty," Mom said.

"Oh, thank you, thank you, thank you!" I hugged each one of them.

I stood at Snowdrops' shoulder and let her nuzzle my open left palm with her velvety horse lips. I hugged her tightly around her neck. "Hello, my new horse."

"We'll put her next to Diamond Jack's stall, that way you and Allison can be together. I already moved George across the aisle so Snowdrops could have his stall." Stan slid out Snowdrops' brass nameplate from her old stall, which had been next to Lisa's horse's stall, and went to put it on her new stall.

"Do you want to ride her?" Keith asked me. "She's already cleaned up. I can tack her up if you want me to."

"I didn't bring boots or breeches with me," I said. "Can I take her outside to eat some grass, just spend some time with her?"

"She's your horse," Stan said. "You can do whatever you want."

I snapped on a lead rope, unfastened the cross-ties, and led Snowdrops outside. Mom, Dad, and Grandma Leona came along with me. I walked Snowdrops over to a grassy spot near the front ring and let her graze in the late afternoon sun. I put my right arm across her back. She flipped her tail to swish at the flies.

I couldn't wait to tell Allison and Ingrid the super-duper-great news. I finally had a horse of my own.

Questions for the Author

1.) What's your favorite kind of horse? Why?
*I love all types of horses, but if I had to pick a few
favorites I'd probably say it's a toss up between a
Thoroughbred, an Oldenburg, a Dutch Warmblood,
and a Quarter Horse. These breeds are sporting
horses who are generally quiet and good-natured,
with the exception of a Thoroughbred—they can be
high-strung, especially if they are young and off the
race track. I have handled many Thoroughbreds, and
most of them were well-trained and well-mannered. I
prefer a gentle horse breed with a good disposition
and a willing temperament for riding.*

2.) Do you ride English or Western?
*I've ridden both, but I prefer to ride English since I
liked to jump. By English, I mean hunt seat and not
saddleseat. Saddleseat, like when Cassie goes to see
the first horse, Master, that Stan arranged for her
and her dad to try on that first Saturday morning in
"Mystery Horse at Oak Lane Stable," is a different
kind of riding English. It's used for showing off
3- and 5-gaited horses like Saddlebreds and Tennessee Walkers (although these two breeds' gaits are
slightly different). Hunt seat is ridden when jumping
over fences. I used to ride Western when I was young-
er. It was fun to swing up into that big old saddle and
ride all day long with my friend and her pinto pony.
But if I had wanted to jump while riding Western, I
would've gotten stabbed in the stomach with the
saddle horn, which I did once and learned my lesson.*

3.) How many horses have you had?

No horses (yet), but two ponies. My first pony was a Shetland named Briggs. He was older, although I don't remember his exact age. He was a great first pony—friendly and willing to try (almost) everything I wanted to do with him, like jumping. He loved homemade cookies, appreciated everything (except grown men), and looked like a fuzzy teddy bear when his winter coat grew in. My second larger pony was an Arab/Welsh cross named Moby (since he was all white). He was strong and loved to jump over the natural fences I set up along the country paths we rode on. He hated carrots but loved banana skins, ran off with me twice—once through the neighbor's award-winning show flowers—and would roll in the dirt right after I'd given him a bath. I've handled hundreds of horses throughout my life, but I haven't owned any of them.

4.) What are some of your favorite horse stories?

My favorites when I was young were "Black Beauty" by Anna Sewell, "High Courage" by C.W. Anderson, the Black Stallion series by Walter Farley, and the Misty series by Marguerite Henry. As an adult, my favorites are "The Fox in the Cupboard: A Memoir" by Jane Shilling, "The Private Passion of Jackie Kennedy: Portrait of a Rider" by Vicky Moon, "We Walk by Faith & Not By Sight: Life's Lessons Learned from a Bilnd Horse" by Mary E. White, and "Lead with Your Heart: Lessons from a Life with Horses" by Allan J. Hamilton, MD. ANY book with horses in it was always a pleasure for me to read.

5.) Does writing about horses make you want to be with a horse or go to a stable?

Absolutely! Being around horses was such a big part of my life. I miss the sounds and the smells and the joy of being in and around a riding stable. I am able to use my experiences around them to write the horse books, but I still think being around them again would help me add details that I might miss from using only my memories instead of actually interacting with them on a regular basis. Recently, I have started to contact stables in my area to get back on and ride regularly. I think it's time.

6.) Why do you write about horses? Why do you love them so much?

I was born with a deep passion for horses like other people who are born loving cars or fish or rocks—it's something that comes from deep inside a person, an internal compass of sorts. Everything had to be horse or horse-related for me as I grew up. I was fortunate to have had my own ponies, show a neighbor's horse in 4H, then move on to a professional life as a show groom, rider, and riding teacher for two hunter/jumper stables when I was in my early 20s. I also taught lessons and rode on and off throughout most of my life. I recently volunteered at Rides & Reins LLC (a therapy stable in our area) where I groomed, tacked up, and led horses in lessons. Now, I currently write horse books inspired by all of the experiences I've had and hope one day to be able to own a horse or two.

7.) Have you written any other horse books besides *Mystery Horse at Oak Lane Stable*?

Yes. "Gray Horse at Oak Lane Stable" (Book 2) was published September 2020 and "Dark Horse at Oak Lane Stable" (Book 3) will be done by the Spring 2021—completing the Oak Lane Stable Adventures Trilogy. All three books have Cassie and her two best friends, Allison and Ingrid, in them, plus an array of new friends and old riding rivals. It's been my pleasure to write this series for you, dear readers. May you enjoy them and share them with your friends!

ABOUT THE AUTHOR

KERRI LUKASAVITZ IS THE AUTHOR of the middle-grade/young adult novel series, *Mystery Horse at Oak Lane Stable* (Book 1, which won a 2018 Royal Dragonfly Book Award) and *Gray Horse at Oak Lane Stable* (Book 2), with *Dark Horse at Oak Lane Stable* (Book 3) underway.

Kerri has a BFA from MIAD and an MA in Creative Writing/Literature from Mount Mary University. She recently won the 2020 Lakefly Writers Flash Fiction genre, was a semi-finalist in the 2020 Bethlehem Writers Short Story Award, is the recipient of a 2020 residency at Write On Door County, and was the 2019 Hal Prize winner for Nonfiction.

She was born horse-crazy and a book devotee. She owned two ponies as a child, showed in 4H, worked as a show groom, rider, and riding teacher for two hunter/jumper stables, and recently volunteered at a therapy stable. She lives with her husband on her family's Wisconsin farm, where she grew up surrounded by the natural beauty of the Kettle Moraine.

A percentage of the book's sales will be donated to the Midwest Horse Welfare Foundation and the Wisconsin/Washington County Humane Societies.

She invites you to contact her at www.kerrilukasavitz.com.

Author Kerri Lukasavitz